Style
Sisters

Style Sisters

GREEN GODDESSES

Liz Elwes

PICCADILLY PRESS • LONDON

To my parents – for everything.
To the fabulous writer Cathy Hopkins – whose generosity
and kindness is legendary, I will be ever grateful.
To Giles Elwes and my children William, Alice, Thomas and Jamie
for having such interesting lives and giving me so many lines
in the book (I hope you don't mind).
To my own style sisters: Frances Toynbee, Sarah Mower,
Jill Rothwell, Mary Saldanha, Marion Jeffrey, Anne Rands,
Rosie and Olivia McDonnell and Suzanne Vandevelde.
To Clare Elwes. To Johnny, Christine and Anne-Marie.
To Brenda Gardner, Ruth Williams, Melissa Patey and
everyone at Piccadilly for their help, patience and guidance.
To Bernice Green who started it.

First published in Great Britain in 2007
by Piccadilly Press Ltd,
5 Castle Road, London NW1 8PR
www.piccadillypress.co.uk

A catalogue record for this book is available
from the British Library

ISBN: 978 1 85340 925 7 (trade paperback)

3 5 7 9 10 8 6 4 2

Printed in the UK by CPI Bookmarque, Croydon, CR0 4TD
Cover design and text design by Simon Davis
Typeset by M Rules, London

Set in 11.5 Stone Serif

Chapter 1

'Shove off, Carrie! Go and practise snogging your mirror.'

I cannot believe my ears. How *dare* Ned speak to me like that?

Honestly, that is what he has just yelled up at my window. To make it even worse I saw his two saddo friends sniggering behind their hands, like the couple of simpletons they are.

Snogging my mirror?!

Anyone could tell you that I, Carrie Henderson, do not need *any* snogging practice as I have been going out with Jack Harper for weeks and weeks now.

And as if I could care less what Ned and his mates are doing in the garden. Let them run around with Dad's camcorder chucking footballs at each other. I only stuck my head out of my bedroom window to tell them to shut up. I was drying my hair and couldn't hear the song on the radio over their racket.

And it was a song by the LA Alphas, who, if I can get over a teeny-tiny obstacle, I will be seeing soon. They are my favourite band in the whole wide world. I think they are wonderful. In a cool, mature way, of course.

Ned and his mates are doing their weird thing again. Obviously, as I am his big sister, it is my duty to show no interest in him or any aspect of his little Year Seven life. Since his starring role in the school production of *Joseph and his Amazing Wotsit* (where even *I* admitted he was good and said 'Well done!' and stuff) he has become a major pain. Mum says this is nonsense; he has just *gained more confidence*.

And she says it like it's a good thing.

Frankly I thought Ned had more than enough confidence already, therefore any extra can only be seen as excessive. But apparently Mum, Dad and the whole of Boughton High School disagree with me, as a conversation I had at school yesterday afternoon with my bezzie friends proved:

Rani: 'But he was so great, Carrie, he really was.'

Me (in special deadpan tone a more sensitive person would realise meant '*Must* we talk about this *again*?'): 'Yeah, I know.'

Chloe: 'I had no idea he could sing like that. Did *you*? Honestly, I just had *no* idea.'

Me: 'Yeah, I know . . .'

Rani: 'Why did you never say? I mean you must hear him singing all the time.'

Me: 'Well, sometimes round the house . . .'

Maddy: 'He could easily go professional. I mean, he could be in a boy band when he's older.'

DID SHE NOT SEE ME SHUDDER? THE HORROR!

Rani (the tactful one): 'What I find so amazing is that you can't sing a note, Carrie, can you? Or act? I mean you have absolutely no performing talent, none whatsoever. Which is sad as you've always wanted to star in a romantic film, haven't you? So how come —?

Me: 'CAN WE TALK ABOUT SOMETHING ELSE, PLEASE!'

So anyone can see what I'm up against at the moment.

I'm going downstairs to make a cup of tea and if I happen to feel like looking out of the window I will. Not because I'm interested in what Ned is doing, but because it is a free country.

10.35 a.m.

Well. That was boring.

Out of the kitchen window I could see the following:

Ned's friend Sam holding a camcorder. He pointed it at our apple tree.

Mikey standing behind him, holding a football.

Sam shouting, 'Action!'

Ned emerging from behind the tree. Casual-like.

Mikey lobbing the ball as hard as he could at his head.

Ned falling to the ground moaning theatrically.

Sam saying, 'Cut'.

All three boys gathering around the camera and peering into replay.

They mutter, sigh, and then they do it all over again.

I'm not going to ask. I am going to meet Chloe and Rani instead. We have important business to discuss.

8.10 p.m.

Frustrating day.

Have discussed important business with Chloe and Rani but we have not solved our teeny-tiny problem.

Which is: how can Chloe and I get hold of one hundred pounds each? And quite soon.

It is vital that we manage to do this. The LA Alphas are coming to Wembley Arena. All tickets sold out in less than two hours (and I should know because that's how long I was trying to get through for). But Sasha Dooley's mum managed to get two for her birthday and she doesn't even want them! Sasha Dooley is the coolest girl in our class and is always way ahead of the times. Now that the LA Alphas have a fan base of more than three people looking on an obscure site on the Internet, she is so over them. Her boyfriend is nineteen and plays in a band called Scum Disease. I need say no more.

'Does that make *you* uncool?' Rani asked. 'Not being so much ahead of the times like Sasha, but pretty much living in the here and now?'

'I don't care,' I said, 'Sasha's disdain is my gain.'

'Imagine not wanting two tickets. Two precious tickets . . . precious tickets . . .' Chloe sighed, doing a good impression of Gollum from *The Lord of the Rings*.

'Yes, and imagine selling them to get a new guitar instead.'

'But a hundred pounds,' Chloe wailed. '*Each*. It might as well be a million.'

I felt sorry for Chloe because, since her parents split up, money has been very tight for her family. She doesn't get a lot of treats, but luckily she's fantastic at discovering clothes in second-hand shops and looking stunning in them. But they never go on holiday or anything. Her brother Jim, who has Down's Syndrome, goes away with his special school, but Chloe didn't go anywhere last year and she hasn't mentioned going anywhere this year either.

'Still,' I comforted her, 'at least you know your mum *genuinely* doesn't have it. I know my mum and dad *could* find it if they tried. They are just deliberately choosing to deprive me. He works in a bank for heaven's sake – he could borrow it. And even deputy heads earn something. And another thing, if Mum cancelled her gym membership, which she never, ever uses – and must cost thousands – she could easily manage one hundred pounds. I could go to a concert every month. But mention *that* and see what kind of reaction you get. She goes wild.'

Rani looked sceptical. 'I really can't imagine your mum behaving like a wild thing.'

'Yeah, well that's because you don't know her like I do. You try asking if she's been on the treadmill lately and see her reaction. Not pretty.'

'She scared the pants off Doug Brennan in his last detention. She can be tough when she needs to,' Chloe added.

'Exactly. And unfortunately she feels she needs to be tough about the LA Alphas. She thinks being asked to pay one hundred pounds for a thirty-five-pound ticket is daylight robbery. She has no understanding of their rare and valuable nature.'

Rani sighed. 'Well my mum would be the same. Just as well I'm not that into the band, as I know my dreams would be thwarted too. It's like me wanting that iguana for a pet. I begged and begged, but oh no.'

'It's so unfair,' I wailed, 'I *have* begged. I have pleaded. I have said I'll have no pocket money for a hundred years. But no. Ruin my youth, why don't they? Sentence me to a life of regrets and sorrow. Laugh in the face of my pain . . .'

Chloe interrupted. 'Carrie! Stop it. You're making me feel worse.'

'Sorry. Well, I've given it some thought and we have two options left.'

'And they are?'

'Stealing or selling our bodies.'

'Yeeuuch! I'm not doing either,' Chloe said, recoiling.

'Really?' This was disappointing news for me because I had

already assigned Chloe quite a major part in this plan. 'Are you sure, Chloe? As the prettiest girl in the school by a mile I was rather counting on your support in the selling your body area. I'm sure you could do it. You know, for the greater good.'

Chloe grabbed a cushion off her bed and banged it down on my head.

'See, you're a natural. Some boys might be really into that kinky stuff.'

But in spite of the fact I was almost certain we could get Doug Brennan to pay a fiver for just one kiss, she wouldn't consider it.

It is this sort of refusal to sacrifice oneself for the common good that I find very hard to understand.

9.30 p.m.

Have been downstairs to have one last attempt to persuade Mum and Dad to cough up, but just got further dogged resistance to my pleas. I don't understand it. I said I would be their total slave and do whatever they said forever and ever. They turned it down. It's as if they don't believe me or something.

'What do *you* have that they could possible want?' said Ned. 'You need talent, good looks, an amazing voice . . .'

I rose and headed for the kitchen door, where I stopped, turned, and said with great dignity, 'Prat'.

Which I have to admit was a bit pathetic and not up to my usual standard. I am putting it down to stress. I am not going to give up. I am going to think and think and think. I have sneaked a whole packet of chocolate digestives out of the kitchen. Even if it takes all night, I am not going to bed until I have *a plan*.

 CARRIE'S TIP: • • • • • • • • • • • • • • • • • •

You don't need to go to a gym to exercise off a chocolate biscuit. Just walking or cycling around the block three times a week will make a difference to your energy levels. Even tidying your room and sorting your stuff out is better than just sitting there doing nothing. And moving around eases stress and tension.

Chapter 2

I have a plan.

My imaginary future therapist, Dr Jennings, would be so proud. Everyone thinks that Rani will be Prime Minister because she is so clever and organised, but hey! When it comes to not giving up and that try, try, try again stuff – look no further than yours truly and a packet of chocolate digestives. Not a whole packet, of course – as if I'm that greedy! Ned stole what was left in the packet this morning. He ate it in one bite on the way to the car before going to PC World with Dad.

You would think I would not feel like breakfast after my restless night, but brainwork makes you hungry, so I accepted Mum's offer to make me a sausage sandwich. I am six foot tall and so need regular feeding. Actually Rani is tiny and eats twice as much as anyone else I know, so perhaps that theory doesn't hold up.

Mum said casually into the frying pan, 'Where's Jack this weekend?' Boyfriend radar still blip blip blipping away. Why do parents even *try* to act cool about this sort of thing? I know she's hanging on my every word. Why not shine the interrogation light in my face and slap the torture gear out on the table and have done with it?

I sighed so she would know that:

a) This *was* an invasion of my personal life.

b) I was bestowing a personal favour on her by giving her any information on this subject.

'He's gone to London to see his mum.'

'Is she still with that, er . . . new friend?'

'You mean that lord she ran off with? As far as I know.'

'It must be tough on Jack now his mother lives in France with that man most of the time.'

'Mmm.'

'Just him and his dad rattling around Pitsford Hall together.'

'They get on pretty well.'

'His dad is a huge support to the school. He's so generous. He has paid for all the food for the staff end-of-term barbecue. I see Jack's chosen to do business studies as one of his AS-levels. I wonder if he wants to go into the family businesses with his dad?'

'I've absolutely no idea, Mum, what with him being sixteen and all and possibly *not having worked out his entire future yet*. Anyway, I think it is an outrageous abuse of your power to check out what AS-levels my friends are doing! Please resist the temptation to use your deputy head privileges to spy on my boyfriend. Anyway, he might be a musician . . . he loves his guitar and writing songs.'

Mum wrinkled her nose. 'Very hard to make a living at it, though,' she said, and forked a couple of sausages on to my plate.

Actually, I know Mum really likes Jack. He gets her real smile when he comes round. If my mum doesn't think you're a nice person, you get her fake smile and I can tell you that it is quite a chilling experience and you better start working your socks off to get an upgrade.

'Mum?'

'Mmm.' She was eating a sausage.

'What's Ned up to? You know with Dad's camcorder, in the garden?'

'Do you know, I have *absolutely* no idea. I was hoping you might be able to tell me. Dad asked him this morning, but he just muttered something vague about a school project. But I know that can't be quite right . . . He said it was a "sort of film". Dad's going to work on getting it out of him this morning. Which reminds me, I need to check that Mrs McGuy is taking the school camera on your trip to Devon. It's coming up so soon, and there's so much to organise.'

'It's going to be brilliant. Year Nine running wild in the great outdoors. Might make up for the postponement of the Black and White Ball.'

Mum's face clouded. 'Yes, that leak in the hall roof has been a disaster. Roll on the new theatre block being finished. Anyway, what are your plans for today?'

I had my own reasons for not telling Mum about my brilliant idea for making my fortune but I did have something else exciting I could tell her about.

'We're going to Maddy's. Her mum has had the most amazing ultra-modern gym installed with all the latest equipment and, the best, best, best part – a hot tub! It's all finished and her mum says we're allowed to go and use it all.'

Mum looked thoughtfully at the last piece of sausage at the end of her fork and put it down.

'That's nice.' She sighed. 'I suppose I should get to *my* gym today. I haven't been for a little while.'

Little while! Over six months and counting, I think. But I knew better than to say a word on *that* subject.

11.35 a.m.

Despair!

I have just spent forever trying on suitable outfits for visiting ultra-modern-gym-with-hot-tub. This outfit does not exist in my wardrobe.

I am also looking for a suitable *body* for visiting ultra-modern-gym-with-hot-tub. I do not appear to have this either.

What I've got is too white and too long, my legs are shapeless and bendy and my bosoms are not bosomy enough. However, they are obviously more bosomy than when I last wore my blue spotty bikini. Mum has heartlessly refused to dash me immediately into Barney's department store in town to buy me a bigger one. So now I will have to wear the fluorescent red nylon hideousness that is my Boughton High swimming costume. My ultra-modern-gym-with-hot-tub wardrobe now consists of:

1) *Aforementioned Boughton High cossie.*
2) *A greyish sports vest. (Result of white wash meets black sock incident.)*
3) *Ned's new hoodie top that I have just stolen from his room and will have to smuggle out, because if he sees me in it I will surely die.*
4) *My old tracky-bums, which are now three inches too short. I decided to cut them shorter for a trendier 'long shorts' look but didn't do it very well and now I look like an extra from* Pirates of the Caribbean.

I just hope Maddy's dad, Daniel Van de Velde, isn't around to see me. As one of the world's leading writers and influences on fashion, I'm guessing I'm not going to be starting any trends here.

Cannot wait to tell everyone about the great idea.

9.25 p.m.

Even though I am in quite a lot of pain I am still in a good mood. Dr Jennings is going to admire this quality. Braveness. I have decided that I have a lot of it in my personality. I know Rani would say that I showed a lot of braveness this afternoon when I pressed the wrong button on the treadmill and I fell off at a hundred miles an hour. But this is not really what I mean. However, the fact every muscle in my body is in agony and I am still writing this is pretty courageous.

Maddy's house is always a treat to visit and luckily her dad was in Los Angeles and not around to see my ultra-modern gym, etc. outfit. Her place is an architect-designed dream, with walls of white and huge glass pieces and a long pale green pool in front of it that reflects the house. It's been in magazines and now, in one of the basement areas, they've built this gym. It's got smooth limestone walls, bright overhead lights on steel wires and a sort of funky black rubber floor where the machines are. The hot tub area is separated from the gym by a long pale blue-green sheet of glass and it's all built in the same pale stone. There are piles of enormous white fluffy towels everywhere as well. I spotted the superior quality of the towels in Maddy's house on my very first visit. Well, superior everything really. I'm not jealous though. I've recently had two weeks of a very posh French exchange girl called Marie-Camille living with us who was very sneery about my house at first. I learned from *that* experience that it's the people that live in the house that make it great, not the furniture. I think that our Paris Princess realised that too by the end. (Though if anyone offered me a gym and hot tub I probably wouldn't say no – it would be rude to refuse.)

Anyway, must finish soon as my arms are hurting writing in this position.

When we all got into the hot tub I decided it was the moment to tell them my plan.

'Burgers?' Rani shrieked. 'Burgers?'

'Yes indeed,' I replied calmly.

'Burgers in school?' Chloe looked confused.

'Yes, burgers in school, during lunch-time. Everyone will go crazy for them. We'll make a fortune.'

Maddy had her serious look on. 'And where are you going to get them from?'

And this was my masterstroke.

'Our fridge freezer. There are tons in there, organic ones, and buns. Mum bought them for the staff end-of-term barbecue. Jack's dad donated the funds. She won't notice a few going missing at first and then I'll replace them.'

'How are you going to cook them?' Rani asked. 'It's the end of June, the radiators aren't even on to warm them up.'

But I was ahead of her. 'I'm going to use my mum's lean mean grilling machine. You know, they advertise them on the telly all the time. She bought one and she never uses it. You just plug it in.'

'Where?' Rani was peering beadily at me across the bubbling water.

'Er . . . The girls' toilets?' I said hesitantly, possibly showing I hadn't thought of every angle *quite* yet.

'Oh yuck no!' she screamed. 'Disgusting, revolting and unhygienic. I'm going to be sick . . .' She sank beneath the bubbles, then resurfaced. 'And anyway, no electrical sockets.'

I had to admit she was right. Quick rethink needed. 'What about the changing rooms?'

Rani screwed up her eyes. 'Could *just* work. But it's a pretty dodgy plan. We could easily get caught.'

'I'd put people on lookout.' I gave a hopeful smile at Maddy and Chloe across the steamy cauldron.

Chloe looked serious. 'I have to say, Carrie, I do not like this plan AT ALL. I think it sounds seriously flawed.'

'On quite a few levels,' Maddy said, nodding.

'Me too,' Rani echoed. 'No offence, but I don't think it's one of your best ideas. I don't want to do it either. Too risky. Maddy and I want to help you get to the concert but that plan is destined for disaster.'

I looked at Chloe. 'Do you want to go to the LA Alphas or not?'

'I *do*. But can't we think of something else? There must be something. I think I'd rather do anything else.' She caught my eye. '*Apart* from snogging Doug Brennan, that is.'

'Then it will have to be Plan B,' I said firmly.

'Oh God. No. Not one of your Plan Bs,' Rani groaned and her head disappeared again under the gurgling bubbles. I patiently waited for her to emerge.

'No, it's good. Listen. I could sell my advice to people in the school. You know how good I am at that sort of thing. You know, bit like an agony aunt. People could come and tell me their problems and I use my wisdom to help them and you can all help me out too . . .'

There was a pause.

'Burgers it is then,' Rani sighed.

And everyone was agreed. I have to admit I was expecting a lot more resistance but it just goes to show what a great idea the burger one really was. I'm bringing the burgers and buns into school in my school bag tomorrow. I'll put the grilling machine in my sports bag to sort of balance out the weight. We'd get word around the school, starting with everyone on the bus.

I am *so* the businesswoman of the year. Who knows, one day I might be able to buy myself a house like Maddy's with an ultra-modern-gym-with-hot-tub instead of having a cupboard under the stairs that's full of Ned's old skateboards.

Tomorrow heralds the dawn of my business empire.

RANI'S TIP: • • • • • • • • • • • • • • • • •
Chlorine from pools and hot tubs is not great for hair. Either wear your hair up or in a swimming cap. Frequent dips in the pool can give blond hair a greenish tinge. If this happens, putting tomato ketchup on your hair for fifteen minutes can help get it back to its normal colour. Personally, I think I'd rather go for the swimming cap!

Chapter 3

Monday 6.30 p.m.

Brilliant day! I am a female financial whiz.

Boughton burgers are go!

Although it wasn't a good start. As soon as I had waved Dad's car off to the station and Mum's off to school, I was in the garage with my head in the freezer stuffing plastic bags with frozen burgers and buns. Thank goodness Mum leaves so early and I get the school bus later. Perfect window of opportunity.

'Whotcha doing, sis?'

I banged my head on the lid of the freezer.

'God, Ned! You gave me a flippin' heart attack! What the hell are you doing here?'

He looked cagey. 'Well, I feel I could ask you the same question. What *are* you doing here?'

'None of your business.'

'Bit peckish, are you?' he said, eyeing my bags.

'I said none of your business.'

'OK, but I have to say I wonder what Mum will do when she realises that the staff end-of-term barbecue might be a slightly *leaner* affair than she imagined. A burgerless barbie. A barbie for the bunless . . .'

'Shut up. You are not going to tell Mum because it's all going to be replaced. She will never know and if you tell her I . . .'

But then, just out of the corner of my eye, I spied his foot beginning to nudge an old bag on the floor by the side of the freezer. He saw me clock this move and lunged, but I was faster and grabbed the bag.

'Ah ha!' I said. And 'Oh ho!' as I pulled out what was in it. (It is hard not to be triumphant when life gives you a break.) 'Dad's camcorder! Planning on taking it into school, were you, when you know if he found out you would be so, so blasted?'

'Give it to me, Carrie. You're going to break it waving it around like that.'

I gave him a level look. I held on to the camera.

'Mmmm. Let me see.' I waved a finger on my free hand between him and me. 'I believe we have a bit of a "let's make a deal" situation going on here, do we not?'

Ned sighed. 'Cool with me.'

I handed him back the camera.

'Thanks, sis, and anyway, what are you going to do with those?' He pointed at the plastic bags.

'I'm going to get to see the LA Alphas. And while we're into the questioning thing, what are *you* going to do with Dad's —'

Ned was scuttling for the door, putting the camera bag into his backpack.

'Got to dash, sis, got a bus to catch.'

I knew he wouldn't have told Mum about the burgers even if I hadn't found the camera, but I had spared myself a lot of low-level Ned irritation. And that really was the hardest part. The rest was easy-peasy.

On the bus on the way home, even Rani had to admit that it had gone amazingly well.

'Sixteen burgers! That's not bad, Carrie. I regret having the slightest doubt about this plan. You are going to make a fortune.'

'Thank you. I will admit that we were blessed with the news that Miss Gooding hasn't reappeared from her clubbing weekend in Prague. It is her break duty this week and so no one's patrolling the changing rooms. Now the word is out, I think they'll be queuing around the back of the showers tomorrow.'

'We could have sold more today if your mum's lean mean grilling machine could cook more than two at a time.'

'True, but the great news is that Maddy's mum has one too. Maddy's going to bring it in tomorrow. That means we double our income.'

Maddy leaned over across the aisle.

'Happy to help you out. But I have to ask – have you worked out how much the burgers and buns are going to cost to replace? Morally I feel I have to ask if I am aiding and abetting this scheme. Organic burgers aren't cheap and your mum is definitely going to notice if you take even more. Are you sure your prices cover that cost? They seemed pretty cheap.'

'Absolutely. Done all that.'

Rani shot me a look, but I ignored it and pretended to look casually out of the bus window at the passing trees.

The trouble with questions like Maddy's is that you don't really want to think about them, because once you have thought about them, and you have worked out the answer, it might not *exactly* be the answer you were hoping for.

Rani leaned into me and whispered, 'Put the prices up.'

I turned to face her.

'Put the prices up tomorrow,' she continued. 'People will pay;

they are organic and deliciously popular. If you put up the prices you can cover your costs and still make a profit. Put the price up by one pound each.'

'Put the price up by a pound!' I shrieked.

'What!?' Jet had turned round and was eyeing us suspiciously through her mascara-laden eyelashes. She was still a strange orange hue. The effect was almost tiger-ish. We had put on a fashion show recently and Jet's skin colour had been one of the most vivid memories of the evening. Apart from Chloe's design winning, of course. 'Put the price of what up by a pound?'

'Our delicious lunch-time burgers,' Rani replied.

'No way! I heard about them. I was going to come and get one tomorrow. Why are they going up by a pound? Screaming daylight robbery, if you ask me. Why were they cheaper today?'

There was a slight pause while Rani gave her a level stare. 'Introductory offer,' she said firmly, crossing her arms. She turned to talk to Maddy across the aisle.

Maybe this is why she will be Prime Minister and I won't.

Must go, Mum is calling me down to eat. Will finish what happened with Jet later.

8.30 p.m.

Back in my room.

Just had two helpings of lasagne as part of my calorie-controlled diet. The calorie-controlled bit was the salad I had with it.

In spite of our deal, Ned could not resist asking Mum, 'Mum, when were we going to have burgers again? Carrie is *such* a *huge* fan.'

So I replied, 'Yes, and then maybe you could *film* me eating them, Ned. Hey? Hey?'

Dad looked quite worried and said, 'Have they both been over-working?'

And Mum laughed in a mirthless way and said that would be the day. I got back up here as quickly as I could.

After Rani said about the introductory offer thing, Jet narrowed her eyes but thought better of carrying on the conversation and went back to chatting to Melanie about their favourite subject. Boys. Actually they do have another one – Victoria Beckham and their chances of marrying a footballer. Which is pretty much the same thing as boys when you think about it.

Jet was saying, 'It's not like you're not pretty or anything, Melaneee. And you've got a great personality.'

I would beg to differ there.

'I *know*,' Melanie bleated. 'But how are we going to *meet* any?'

And I could see their dilemma. For two fourteen-year-old girls at Boughton High, getting a date with Premier League footballers might well be considered a bit of a challenge.

'I've got a plan.' Jet smirked at Melanie.

'Really?' Melanie gasped. 'A plan to get us to meet Manchester United players and the like?'

Jet winced slightly. 'Not quite, but nearly. And if my plan works I'm sure it won't take long for us to use our connections to meet the top players . . . We'll be shopping in Milan with the best of them before you know it.'

'That would be so brilliant,' Melanie sighed. 'How though?'

'Not saying just yet, but I'm sure I'm right about it. I swear by the end of this term I will have scored us a place in the changing rooms after a big football match. Since we are both young, free and single, it's time we both found ourselves decent boyfriends instead of the sad cases in this school.'

Jet had recently been disappointed in love by the school player, Chris Jones. Even I had fallen briefly (very briefly) for his charms, before I realised what a jerk he was and got together with Jack. Chris was now going out with Jennifer Cooper, who rarely let him out of her sight. For this reason, Jet had obviously given up on him and was thinking about pastures new.

I listened with interest to this conversation. Obviously Jet was in dreamland about being a footballer's girlfriend, but I was interested in the concept of looking for love, because, absolutely not in an interfering way or anything, I am on the lookout for romance for one of my friends. And that friend is Maddy. You see, I have Jack, Chloe has Tom, Rani is best mates with Kenny and seems very happy with just that at the moment. I wouldn't dare try and guess who she might fancy anyway, she has weird taste. Maddy, on the other hand, was obviously given a hard time at her American school about being on the large side and was pretty lonely there. She only arrived here at the beginning of term and now she's running several times a week, she looks a hundred times better – more sort of curvy and fit. And she's very pretty, in a Kelly Osbourne kind of way. I think she must at least be *thinking* about the boys now. I had thought she liked Joe Carter in Jack's year, and he might be a possibility – but now their GCSEs are over, he's not around so much and I heard he was seeing a girl in his year, Steph Barker. He's super popular, hunky and captain of his year's football team. I think that maybe (as I am sure this will be Maddy's first proper boyfriend) she should start with something a bit more manageable anyway. And I'm thinking Nathan in our class. He is such a gentle, nice boy. Average looking. No trouble at all. I am going to stop biting my nails and conference call Rani and Chloe about it.

9.30 p.m.

I wish I hadn't bothered.

'A starter boyfriend!' Rani shrieked.

'What's wrong with that idea?' I protested. 'Nathan is such a sweetheart. Not bad looking. Medium height, light brown hair, friendly face. Not exactly an alpha male as they say . . . he wouldn't be leading Scottish tribes in olden times or getting the part as James Bond, but that doesn't mean to say he can't make someone a perfectly good boyfriend.'

'A boyfriend for beginners . . .' I could tell Chloe was being judgemental simply by her tone. 'And what happens when she's passed her boyfriend dating test? Can she throw away her L-plates and run around the streets, free to move on to whoever she wants?'

'And attempt the dangers of the bus shelter alone with a Year Eleven: the boyfriend equivalent of reversing into a very small parking space?' Rani added.

'Oh ha very ha. Look, what I mean is, if you haven't had a boyfriend before, you might want to begin with someone not too challenging.'

'Carrie?' It was Rani's turn to sound serious.

'Mmmm?'

'That is a very, very patronising idea. It's patronising to Nathan and it's patronising to Maddy. I am sure they are both more than capable of looking after themselves in the love department.'

I pursed my lips tightly for a moment, then I said, 'Well, that's your opinion, but I think if we look at the evidence I may have to disagree with you. *Is* either of them going out with anyone? No? I don't think so! Mmmm . . . ladies, you see. I rest my case.'

Rani tried another tack. 'I thought he liked Jennifer Cooper anyway?'

I sighed.

'He did have a bit of a crush on Jennifer, but now she's completely obsessive about Chris, I'm hoping he might realise that's hopeless and be looking around again.'

I heard Chloe take a deep breath. 'Carrie, you must promise, promise, promise, not to interfere or do any of your mad stuff about this.'

Rani was right behind her. 'Promise?'

'Please,' Chloe went on. 'It's a really, really bad idea, on so many levels. Trust us. Please. Promise never to mention it again.'

'What! I'm not allowed to even *mention* anything? I'm not allowed to *express* myself at all? A girl's allowed to just *say*, isn't she? We did live in a democracy last time I looked. Or was I off sick the day that they cancelled free speech?'

Rani was not to be sidetracked. 'Crappiest idea to come out of crap-ideas town for quite a while, Carrie. Seriously. You do not have a good track record on this. Promise you won't do anything?'

I sighed deeply. 'God. OK-aaay. If you're going to get so stressed about it.'

I was obviously on my own in thinking this Nathan thing was a good plan. Well, I would do it on my own then. 'OK,' I concurred. 'My lips are sealed, I will not mention one word about it ever again to you. Not a word.'

I have to accept that no one else cares about bringing love and happiness into people's lives. Which is very, very sad when you think about it.

CHLOE'S TIP: ●
If you bite your nails, like Carrie, and want to stop, try investing in some false ones. You can buy them in a big chemist's and they don't cost a lot. Your teeth won't like the feel of the fake nails and it will help you kick the habit. You will also see how great it is having fabulous-looking nails and never want to bite again. (Well, that's the theory anyway.)

Chapter 4

Getting ready for school.

Mum has just told me some interesting news.

I had just wandered past Mum and Dad's room on the way back to my mirror – for some extra beautification – due to seeing Jack after school today. Mum was lying on the floor in her bra and pants (they actually sell them that big?) slowly lowering her legs to the floor. Her hand gave me a cheery wave but the puffed-out cheeks on her face told another story. She gestured for me to wait. I wanted to put her out of her misery and say, 'Look, Mum, I don't know why you worry about exercising – a few minutes' puffing on the floor waving your legs around isn't really going to make much inroad into well over forty years of accumulated poundage. And we won't even mention the cellulite. Dad's no oil painting, why bother?'

However, I do not do this. I cannot be sure she would take it in the spirit with which it was intended. She can be very over-sensitive sometimes.

She collapsed back on to the bedroom carpet and told me the good tidings. Miss Gooding has broken her leg! This is not, of course, good news in itself. Actually pretty bad news for Miss Gooding I would guess, but very good news for the burger business. Apparently she fell off a dance podium whilst doing her boogie thing in a club in Prague. I wondered why we had the lumpy toffee-chewing supply teacher yesterday. They don't know when Miss G will be back. Mum has applied to the teaching agency she uses when desperate and apparently they have come up with a very experienced geography teacher. Mum is relieved because of the school trip (our outward-bound adventure just before the end of term) – Miss Gooding was taking us. Lumpy supply teacher can barely cross the room without gasping for breath, let alone dangle on a piece of rope from a cliff top. So Mum *is* desperate. Now we will go with Miss Gooding's replacement. And Mrs McGuy, of course. And Mr Goodge, the geriatric physics teacher and wannabe DJ. Miss Gwatkins will be the only member of staff coming with us who is under a hundred years old. I expect the new geog teacher will bear a striking resemblance to a tortoise as well.

Front door has just gone. Mum has left for work. Must go and grab more burgers and buns.

It is hard work being a top businesswoman.

8.45 p.m.

School seemed to go on forever today, but at last it was over and we met the boys in the Coffee Bean. Very exciting to see Jack. It is always very exciting to see Jack. Our passion does not dim with the passage of time – it's been weeks now.

'I hear you're making a killing with your greasy burger bar,' Tom launched in, in his usual charming way.

I pulled myself up straighter. 'If, by that, you are referring to our thriving organic alternative lunch option, then yes. It's going brilliantly. Now Maddy has brought in her mum's grilling machine, we are seriously in business.'

'Think you are going to make enough money to get those tickets?' Kenny asked.

'If we carry on like this, who knows? We sold twenty-seven today. So Sasha says she's not going to put the tickets on eBay yet.'

'Twenty-seven!' Jack gasped. 'How did you manage to smuggle twenty-seven burgers and buns into school?'

'Yes, well. I had help. Ned agreed to take a load of buns in his PE kit bag.'

Jack raised his eyebrows. 'Ned? Doing you a big favour? What was the deal?'

'Free burger for him and his mates Mikey and Sam.'

'Ooh hard bargain. Are all the Hendersons so ruthless in business?'

I flicked my hair back over my shoulder. 'I am beginning to feel that there may be some sort of instinctive know-how in my blood.'

Rani laughed in an unnecessary sort of way.

Jack continued, 'It's just that I've never really thought of you and Chloe as materialistic people. And now getting people to part with their cash seems to be a big preoccupation.'

'We need money for those tickets,' I explained.

'And selling junk food to school kids is OK with you, is it?'

'Junk food! How dare you! It's not junk food. They are grilled organic burgers. I simply saw a niche in the market. We are supplying a demand.'

'But there is no *real* demand,' said Jack, frowning.

'Are you kidding?' I replied. 'You should see the queues.'

'No, what I mean is that they could all have their school dinners, which are already paid for. In effect they are paying twice – once for the dinner they don't eat and again for the burger. It's a lot of wasted food in uneaten school meals . . .'

'We don't force them to eat our burgers. It's up to them what they spend their money on.' This conversation was not going quite as I had imagined.

'I suppose.' Jack shrugged. 'But it's a bit like mobile phones. Most people have got them, but they still want the new one when it comes out. But we don't *need* them, do we? Or to try the latest burger from the fast food chains. By the way, where are these burgers coming from?'

I chose to ignore this part of the question.

'Yes, well, this isn't like burgers from a fast food chain. They are preservative and chemical free.'

'Probably no more exploitative than Sasha asking you for one hundred pounds each for a thirty-five-pound ticket,' Jack sighed.

'Hello!? A massive lot less exploitative-thingy,' I huffed.

Jack frowned and he ran his long fingers through his dark hair. 'It's just that it's all basically stuff that you don't really need. The kids at school don't need the burgers and you don't need the tickets to the LA Alphas. You *want* them. Which is a different thing. I suppose neither of them is that important. Just might be good to be raising money in a less wasteful way for a better cause . . .'

I was feeling quite hot and bothered by now. I had imagined Jack would be impressed by my success, not be all weird and preachy about it. But maybe it is because his dad has loads of money so poverty is not something he would really understand. I could see he was making Chloe and Rani feel bad about it as well. I couldn't have that. That might lead to them pulling out of the plan.

I changed the subject. 'I wonder what Miss Gooding's replacement will be like?'

Rani sat back and sighed. 'Ah, the supply geography teacher. Now let me see. She'll be a dreary thirty-something with heavy thighs in Marks and Spencer stretch black trousers and a too-tight bold-print wrap-over top with some oversized necklace and a short haircut that looks like she did it with the kitchen scissors at home, but she thinks looks "funky".'

'No, she won't,' I interrupted. 'It's not a "she", it's a "he".'

'God, even worse. He'll wear elephant cords and a yellowing nylon shirt and smell vaguely of fags and greasy hair. And have dandruff.'

Now it was Jack's turn to sit back. 'Yuck! Rani where do you get that from?'

She shook her head. 'Years of bitter experience at Boughton High. You've only been here a short while. You wouldn't know about what we've had passing through our classrooms over the years.'

Jack held my hand under the table and I was glad because I was worried that he didn't like me so much now I was a capitalist and exploiting the masses. I would explain to him how wrong he was later.

'And when are you off on your school trip with this lovely scented man?' he asked.

'The last week of term.'

Tom's large, round face creased into a grin. 'Oh yes, the school trip. I remember it well. What larks we had. You're going to the one in Devon, aren't you?'

We nodded.

'Yeah, what about this trip?' Maddy intervened. 'What happens there? I've seen all the stuff the school sent out. It looks cool.'

'It is, you'll have a great time. Chris Jones was in his element, showing off, dangling from ropes from high places, etc. . . By the way, rumour has it that Chris is cooling off your friend Jennifer – big time.'

I saw Jack's brow frown for a fraction of a second. He knows I'm not in the slightest bit interested in Chris, but I think it still annoys him that I once was – for that very, very short time – a little bit keen on him. And he knows that Chris asked me if we could get back together recently and that hasn't endeared him to Jack either.

Tom continued, 'You get to try loads of things you've never done before, like abseiling and stuff like that. And they have a big party on the beach on the last night.'

Maddy grinned. 'Sounds great.'

'It is. Good place for getting a snog as well.'

Chloe shot him a fake-horrified glance.

'Oh God no! Not me, but if you fancy someone in your year, that's the best opportunity for getting together. Quite a few people in our year began their relationships by grabbing a quick kiss in the dunes behind the beach.'

'Mercy, Tom!' Rani placed her hand on her chest. 'You make it sound *so* romantic!'

I looked at Maddy. I wondered if she was hoping that she was going to get together with someone while we were away. But she was looking at her watch and getting up. She had to get home. Something about not wanting to miss a programme on American TV. They have every cable and satellite channel known to mankind at her house.

Then Jack and I went for a wander back to the bus stop. As Jack had finished his GCSEs he didn't have to wear his school uniform and, to his credit, he didn't even act the tiniest bit ashamed that I was stuck in mine. I had rolled up the shirtsleeves and hitched up the skirt as much as I could, but it still wasn't a great look. He was looking tanned now, but those of us still slaving away at school had barely seen the sun. A smattering of tiny freckles across my nose was the only indication that I had been allowed outside at all this term.

I decided not to bring up the subject of my business empire just yet. I had something else I wanted to talk about. 'Jack.' I paused. 'You're a boy.'

He looked down at me and raised an eyebrow. 'Ye-es,' he said slowly. 'I *am* a boy.' He frowned. 'Unless I've been labouring under a massive delusion.'

'OK. So you're a boy. That means you must know what boys like.'

He nodded. 'Go on.'

'I just think that I'd like to know what boys really like . . .'

He gave me a truly wicked grin. 'I have to say that I have not the slightest idea where you're going with this, Carrie – but it's sounding very promising.'

'No, listen. You might know, *as a boy*, what sort of girls *other* boys might like.'

He put on a thoughtful expression. 'I might know what sort of girls *other* boys might like. Mmmm. I think you are going to have to explain further and please feel free to go back to the "you must know what boys like" bit. Because that was the bit I liked best. Definitely.'

'Stop it. You know what I mean.'

'I really don't.'

'I mean, could you tell what sort of a girl another boy might go for? I don't know, someone like Nathan in our year, for instance. Who do you think he might ask out, be interested in . . .'

He stopped walking and pulled my arm gently towards him.

'Carrie,' he growled in a warning tone, 'what are you up to?'

'Nothing! Honestly nothing at all. I was just thinking about Maddy and thinking that she hasn't had a boyfriend and maybe she might be vaguely thinking that she might want one . . .'

'Has she told you this?'

'God no! Maddy would never discuss something like that. She's so private and independent.'

'And maybe that's how she would like to stay.'

'But what if she does like someone and she doesn't know our English ways of going about these things and needs some help?'

'She's from America, Carrie! Not the sweeping steppes of Outer Mongolia. I'm sure she won't be embarrassing herself trying to rub noses or leaving gifts fashioned out of whale blubber in people's desks to indicate her interest . . . Los Angeles is pretty sophisticated, you know.'

I gazed casually up at the sky. Jack got my hands and put them in his, like we were both praying. He looked down into my face.

'Now, Carrie. We've been here before, haven't we? The interfering in people's love lives thing. Because we've talked about this and me and Dr Jennings are in total agreement.' (Damn, why did I ever tell him about her.) 'Don't go there.'

So I did the only sensible thing in the circumstances and leaned forward and gave him a long kiss.

This resulted in two things. One, a very enjoyable experience. And two, it distracted him from the conversation.

Me too, but I held on to enough reason, after I had floated back down to earth, to realise that Jack was not going to help me out either.

So we talked about the up and coming school trip instead and he asked if Mr Nylon Shirt had arrived and I said he'd be starting tomorrow. I started to try to put him right on the burger scheme thing but Jack stopped me and said we would have to 'agree to disagree'. And that's no good, when it is obvious that I am right. I realised that I was on my own as far as my new business venture was concerned as well. It is right what they say about being a successful businesswoman.

It can be lonely at the top.

 MADDY'S TIP: ●

If, like me, you do exercise and don't have time for a shower, always use a cleansing wipe to remove sweat and oil from your face. Clean skin will reduce the chances of spots and blackheads.

If you do get a pre-party spot, apply toothpaste to it the night before. Overnight it will help dry out the skin and reduce redness around the area.

Chapter 5

Wednesday 5.45 p.m.

Massive excitement.

Miss Gooding's replacement arrived. Games was cancelled. Huzzah! We had double geog instead, to make up for the lesson with the lumpy supply. Mrs McGuy sent us down to the geog room from register. She said nothing about the new teacher, but I noticed her nostrils were on half flare.

What can I say? Mr Nylon Shirt he was not.

He walked into the classroom. Excuse me? Did I say 'walked'? No, no, no! 'Walked' doesn't nearly cover it. He 'strode', 'sprang', possibly 'lightly bounded' into our geography lesson. Closely followed by a rather flushed Miss Gwatkins gazing up adoringly at his six-foot-two frame. Her eyes were not the only ones on him – the peepers of practically every girl in the class were focused on this new object of interest.

'9M, 9M!' Miss Gwatkins, her peroxide locks all awry, flapped her little hands like a baby seal in an effort to drag some attention her way. 'This is Mr Trent. Mr Trent will be taking you for geography till the end of this term and will be coming on the school trip with me, ooh!' She blushed. 'I mean *us*, next week. We are very grateful to him for stepping in to help out.' She gave him a gushing beam.

He looked slowly around the room.

'I'm very excited to be here.' He had a low, melodious voice, with a slight American accent. 'Thank you for that cool introduction, Miss Gwatkins.' It was his turn to smile slowly at her. She grinned soppily back as if in a trance, before giving a little start. 'Oh yes, right, well, I'll leave you to it then.' And she tripped over the bin on the way out.

I looked over at Rani, who was staring straight ahead with her mouth open. As was Chloe. Mr Trent was not wearing geog-teacher corduroys, but slim black denims with black baseball boots. The same kind that my big brother Max wears. He was not wearing a yellowing nylon shirt either. He unravelled a long thin cotton neckscarf and revealed a faded green, tie-dyed long-sleeved T-shirt. He pulled up the sleeves to expose tanned arms. He draped the scarf over the back of the chair, rummaged in his back pocket and produced a rubber band; he lifted both arms into the air and then ran both hands through his longish curling dark hair, and pulled it back into a thick ponytail, revealing a small silver earring in one ear.

He scanned the room slowly with a pair of dark blue eyes, fringed with dense black lashes. And then he did a daring thing.

In one bound he leapt athletically up on to the teacher's desk. He sat facing us, swinging his long legs to and fro, and leaned forward.

Now this *is* a daring move. It's one we've seen before at Boughton High and it's always risky. Very, very few teachers can pull off this 'being cool with the kids' stuff without looking stupid and quite frankly, you feel embarrassed for them. But I have to give it to Mr Trent, he got away with it.

'So,' he said, nodding seriously, 'here we all are.'

This couldn't be denied so no one said anything.

'OK, now, before we do anything else, who can tell me, what

is your opinion of geography? What does it really mean to you, as an individual? Let's just throw some ideas in the air here . . .' He gazed at the spectacle of 9M briefly trying to get their brain cells around this and then, one by one, abandoning the struggle.

Mr Trent began to gesticulate with his brown arms. 'You mean that no one sees how important it is to understand the environment, the way we live, our effect on the planet?' A sharp intake of breath. 'Are you telling me,' (dramatic pause) 'that no one here *cares*?'

I could see the expression on Rani's face. She was bursting to show she cared. She just wasn't quite sure how.

He closed his eyes and held up a hand. 'OK, you guys. Maybe I am rushing things. You got to get used to a new aura, a new vibe, and maybe I'm not giving you enough space.'

I saw Zack roll his eyes at Connor.

'As we're going to be spending some time with each other perhaps I should start by telling you a little bit about' – Mr Trent gestured towards his manly frame – 'myself. Yes, I am a teacher. Yes, I guess I'm going to be just that little bit different from what you're used to. I've been teaching for a few years now, but not in a school anything at all like this . . .' He looked around with a slight shudder.

Sarah Li put her hand up. 'Where have you been teaching?'

'In the school where I've been, the kids make the rules. I guess you could say that they enjoy . . .' – he made quotation mark wiggles with his fingers – '. . . an *alternative* education experience.'

Zack put his hand up. 'Where is it?'

Mr Trent smiled. 'It's in California. It's an experimental school, called Rainbow Ridge. It was set up by a group of people who were sort of against rules and for freedom and creativity. It has its own organic farm and the kids spend a lot of time just being close to the land and enjoying the beauties of the mountains all around them. Natural springs for them – no lounging about in energy guzzling hot tubs . . .'

I saw Chloe and Rani flush guiltily.

'I left a month ago. I knew it was time to come back home and concentrate on my poetry and songwriting. I wanted some space to commit myself to that.'

Zack's hand went up again. 'So what are you doing teaching us?'

Mr Trent looked slightly pained. 'Er, it can take a while to get established as a poet . . . but it's all good, it means I can get my message across, er, even here . . .'

So he had been in America enjoying the beauties of the natural world. The closest we ever got to the beauties of the natural world in our school was the winnowing plain of the sports field and the little huddle of trees laughably known as 'the woods'. Thank goodness we were going to be visiting some real countryside or Mr Trent would probably start to feel very depressed.

Maddy put up her hand. 'Mr Trent?'

He sprang lightly up from the desk and wandered down to Maddy's desk. 'Hey! There's no Mr Trent here. My name is Guy, but the kids in my last school called me "River", and that's what I would like *you* to call me.'

A collective sigh from most of the girls was audible over the collective snort from most of the boys. Connor had found a rubber band and had managed to get some of his hair in it, which was now sticking out horizontally on one side of his head.

'Er, um . . .' Maddy was struggling with this. 'River?'

'Yup!'

'When are we getting the list of equipment that we are going to need for the Devon trip?'

'Right. You need to know stuff like that? Sure, it will be ready tomorrow. Sorry it's been delayed, but what with Miss Gooding being away and me just starting today. Me, I just throw things in a bag and get on the road. Don't like the material goods thing. Should have realised that for you kids it might be important to know what to bring.'

Maddy raised her eyebrows. 'Yes, it is. Thank you, er . . . River.'

'Right! Now I've been here a few minutes I've noticed some things already that have really brought me right down.'

So he *had* noticed the lack of mountains.

'Let me clarify by asking you a question. How much paper do you reckon your school uses in one year? Any ideas?'

Jackie, Miss Brainy, put up a tentative hand. 'Several tonnes?'

'Define "several".'

'Er, five?'

'Five! No! Think again. Twelve point five. Twelve and a half tonnes of paper used by one school. Think about how many schools there are in this country, and then the world . . . doesn't that just frighten you guys to death?'

It hadn't frightened Connor. He had managed to unearth another rubber band and he had a second bunch of hair sticking out on the other side of his head now.

Others took this more seriously and cast their eyes down in shame. You just knew the kids at Rainbow Ridge never wasted paper and probably fashioned their rubbish into rather fetching brooches as well.

Rani put up her hand. 'We do have recycling bins for stuff in the playground.'

'So what's this?' he asked, producing a plastic water bottle that I had seen her drop in the bin on our way into class.

'Why isn't this in the plastic recycling bin in the playground?'

Rani went scarlet.

River's hands pressed together, as if in prayer; he brought them up to his face and he began tapping his mouth thoughtfully. He slowly gazed around at us. He sighed deeply. 'Guys, I can see that we have got a heap of work to do before the end of term. You've got to be *aware*. Please don't make me low by wasting stuff. Every non-recycled piece of paper or plastic wastes our planet's precious energy resources. *Some* people are trying to make a difference.' He put a CD into the computer. 'Let's show you a little more about this wonderful school . . .'

If I'm going to be honest, by the time it had finished I was a little bit sick of those kids at Rainbow Ridge. They all seemed to be very good-looking with no spots. And that wasn't surprising because they only ate the odd organic vegetable and bean from what I could see. The annoying thing was that they managed to look so good. In fact, they were positively glowing as they all held hands and sang a song about how we are all made of starshine. And none more so than a girl with blond plaits and a rainbow-coloured cotton square tied round her neck.

I looked around to make a face at Chloe and Rani but I was shocked to see them staring straight ahead, their eyes aflame with starshine too.

'Totally inspirational, huh?' Mr Trent was nodding at us all.

'Who's the girl with the plaits?' Jennifer asked.

'Meadow. She's exactly the same age as you guys.'

'Everyone, er . . . seemed nice,' Rani offered.

'Oh yeah, truly, the staff and kids at Rainbow Ridge, they had really beautiful spirits.'

Instantly, I sensed nearly every girl in the class acquire a burning desire to achieve a beautiful spirit as well.

'They're very, um, natural-looking, aren't they?' Cara observed.

River looked serious. 'At Rainbow Ridge we believe that inner beauty is the only kind that matters. The cosmetic industry appals me, with its use of chemicals and animal testing. I don't know why anyone would want to use some of those products. You wouldn't paint a butterfly, would you?'

Zack had his hand up. 'What if you're a centipede, though? Wouldn't they look better tarted up a bit?'

'Yes sir, and slugs,' Connor said, frowning. 'You can't say slugs wouldn't look better with a bit of cosmetic help, sir, could you?'

River was looking curiously at Connor's hair. 'What? Er no. No, slugs . . .'

'And what about centipedes?' Zack added.

'Slugs and centipedes are both . . . um . . . just fine as they are.'

'And what about rats, sir?'

But River had gone up to the board and had begun writing. 'OK, we haven't got much time before we go away. We need to get on with the work Miss Gooding has left for you to do. But while I'm here I'd like you all to think about doing a little project, about making a difference to the environment. Gain awareness and get in touch with the natural world . . . like Meadow. Right.

Devon. We'll be exploring one of the most beautiful areas in the country . . .'

'With your gorgeous body by my side.' That was Rani at break, leaning against her locker. She had a soppy expression on her face, as had most of the female contingent of our class.

'He's so, he's so . . .' Chloe's hands twisted round her dark curls as she tried to find the words.

'Gorgeous,' Rani sighed.

'So gorgeous that God wants him for heaven's boy band?' I offered.

'No! Well yes, that too, but that's not what makes him so . . . interesting. It's his passion, Carrie. His total body and soul commitment to saving the planet. It was so powerful, you could feel its strength . . .'

'Are you sure you're talking about saving the planet here?' I ventured.

'Shut up!' they both said at once.

'Just because you aren't quite as sensitive and in tune with your inner feelings as us, I'd thank you not to belittle our respect. Yes, Carrie, "RESPECT" *is* the word, for River.'

'What! I didn't say anything against him. Was it my imagination or did he actually say, "The earth is the bright blue bobble on the top of God's woolly hat"?'

'No, he blimmin' didn't, Carrie,' Rani snapped. 'And you know it. He said a lot of really moving and thought-provoking things . . .'

'I think the word is "Inspirational",' Chloe sighed.

'Absolutely,' Rani agreed. 'And did you see Jet trying to impress him? With that amount of whale fat on her face. Honestly, it was pathetic. "River, I do love nature so, the sounds of the birds, the wind in the trees ... I often go to the woods near the playing fields at break."'

'True,' I agreed. 'She does.'

'*To have a fag!*' Rani wailed. 'There's River thinking she's breathing in lungfuls of fresh air when she's actually a one woman pollution factory.'

'We have totally got to make him think that we are the greenest girls in the class. We've got to. I want him to know that I have a beautiful spirit,' Chloe sighed.

'Me too,' Rani agreed.

'It's like you two are under a spell.' I waved my hands in a hypnotic way and looked over at Maddy, who was secreting her mum's lean mean grilling machine into her bag ready for our lunch-time session later. 'Is it just me, or am I the only woman in 9M who thinks he's a bit girlie?'

Rani gasped, appalled. 'How can you say that? A BIT GIRLIE! Jennifer said she saw him leaping off his bike when he arrived this morning and hoisting it up on to his shoulder *as if it weighed nothing,* to carry it across the car park. Like an athlete she said he was, like someone doing that French biking thing.'

'The Tour de France.' Chloe nodded. 'He is so fit.' She corrected herself. 'In the athletic, sporting sense of the word of course.'

'Maddy!' I cried. 'Help me out here.'

She laughed. 'Oh, he's OK. Perhaps been in California too long ...'

'OK?! OK?' It was Chloe's turn to be outraged. 'We actually get a member of staff who cares about something important and you say "He's OK"? Maddy, what planet are you on these days? You just don't seem to be concentrating on what's going on any more.'

Maddy smiled. 'I'm sorry, maybe you're right, maybe I have been a bit distracted lately.'

'On what?' I asked, quick as a flash. Maddy's state of mind was very important to me if my plans for her were going to be successful. 'Would it be a boy?'

Maddy flushed. 'What! What makes you think that?'

'Just wondering, you know, Rani and Chloe banging on about Mr Wonders of Nature – even though Chloe has a perfectly good boyfriend and should be ashamed of herself – I was wondering if there was anyone that you might have your eye on, you know, in our class? Possibly?'

Maddy reddened again and said firmly, 'No, there *definitely* isn't.'

This was not the response I was looking for. 'Are you sure?'

'Yes, she obviously is,' Chloe interrupted. 'She's probably busy getting ready for going to Los Angeles for the summer. Stop being such a nosey old bag.'

'Did you know in some religions, Chloe,' I said slowly, 'even *thinking* impure thoughts about someone is considered to be just as unfaithful as snogging their faces off. Did you know that, Chloe?'

'Shut up.'

'Mmm . . . thought so . . .'

Must stop writing now. Need to count the proceeds from today's burger session. For the first time I wish I'd paid more attention in maths.

9.35 p.m.

Still in my room trying to manage the finances of Boughton Burgers.

Rani, Chloe *and* Jack all phoned while I was trying to do this. Rani and Chloe to ask me how we were going to impress Mr Trent (I'm sorry I cannot write River any longer – my hand seizes up with embarrassment). Jack to say he felt bad he cut me off when I had wanted to explain to him about my new financial venture. I had to cut *him* off and say I was busy. I hope running a business empire is not going to come between me and my loved ones.

My multitasking lifestyle is proving quite tiring what with the burgers and thinking about Jack and Maddy and Nathan and everything. But then Dr Jennings would say, 'That's you all over, Carrie. You're a giver.' And I suppose I am.

★ CARRIE'S TIP: •
Plaits like Meadow's can look great, but if you do have long hair, beware of split ends. Nothing can mend them once they start, whatever the hair product people promise you. That's why it's so important to get your hair trimmed regularly. This will stop those thin, wispy ends and keep your hair looking strong and healthy.

Chapter 6

Disaster.

Running a business empire *has* come between me and my loved ones.

I am in my room avoiding the return of Mum. She will be back any minute. Dr Jennings will be horrified that a mere child should be feeling so nervous about seeing their own mother. Parents are supposed to love and support you whatever you do. I might try and remind Mum of this fact when she arrives.

My burger business has collapsed.

And therefore so have my chances of seeing the LA Alphas.

And it is all the fault of Miss Gooding and her dancing ways.

At lunch-time everything was still going according to plan. I was rubbing my hands together with glee because the queue was round the showers and back to the door. The little lights on the grilling machines had just gone on to let you know you can get started, but when I turned round the line of people just evaporated. Leaving Mr T standing there looking horrified. But not as horrified as us. Why had I let Rani skip lookout duty? I hadn't thought it through. Mr Eco-warrior was now on his second day in school and someone had obviously decided he was ready to take Miss Gooding's place on lunchtime patrol.

'What's going on here?'

We stared back in silence.

'Well, someone speak.' He picked up a burger. 'What's this?'

He took a good look. He paled and put it down. 'Meat,' he whispered.

'It's organic,' Rani said in a wavery voice. As if this was going to make a difference.

'You are selling, and I presume you *are* selling, *burgers* to other schoolchildren?'

'Those cows have had lovely lives . . .' Chloe whimpered.

'Pack all this up now, this minute.'

'It's not illegal to eat meat, you know,' I said. (Braveness again.)

Mr T frowned. 'Look, girls, I am fully aware of that, but it *is* against school rules to set up a burger bar in the changing rooms, and to *charge* people for the burgers.' He looked sadly at all of us. 'Can I ask why you feel you had to do this?'

I felt myself blushing.

'We wanted to raise some money,' I said, in a less courageous tone.

'Raise money? What for?'

I shifted uneasily and took a deep breath.

'Tickets. And it was all my idea. Everyone else was just helping to be kind, but it was all my idea . . .'

'Tickets? What for?'

'The LA Alphas,' Chloe whispered. 'And it was for my ticket too. Rani and Maddy had nothing to do with it . . .'

'For a band?!'

Chloe and I nodded.

'Do you know something, there is only one word to describe what I feel about this.' His blue eyes swept across our anxious faces. 'Disappointed.'

'We're not forcing people to eat them. It's not like we're

tricking anyone,' I blustered. Honestly you'd think we were criminals or something.

'But you are using them. You are using people to make profit for yourselves with no regard to the consequences. It's also about health and safety, food poisoning and electrocution to name but a few other reasons. I want you to promise to do something for me.'

We all nodded furiously. Chloe was nearly in tears. I think we all knew our beautiful-spirit rating had plummeted.

'I want you to promise that instead of doing something to make the school environment smell horrible, and waste resources . . .'

We waited expectantly.

'. . . Instead, that you will put the effort into your project and think of ways to make the places you live and work more eco-friendly and show some evidence of caring for the planet. OK?'

More vigorous nodding.

Mr Trent finished with us by saying, 'Now clear all this up and think about what you were doing. You are the future of this planet and your smallest action will affect generations to come.' I felt this was a lot of responsibility for a girl, but I pressed my lips together and just nodded. He walked off.

'Oh God,' wailed Chloe. 'I feel sooo ashamed now. I feel so, so . . . *un*-Rainbow Ridge.'

'Me too,' Rani agreed. 'He really thinks badly of us. He thinks we are moneymaking capitalists, exploiting the common herd at Boughton High. Just like Jack said.'

This made me feel uncomfortable so I went on the defensive.

'The youth of Boughton High weren't complaining. They were queuing round the block.'

'That's not the point . . .' Chloe sighed.

'What *is* the point?' I asked.

'The point is that we now have a mountain to climb for Mr Trent to take us seriously again.'

'I know,' wailed Rani. 'He despises us now.'

'He doesn't despise us!' This was Maddy – the voice of reason. 'He's just a bit, um, shocked, that's all.'

'But I think he does despise you a bit as well.' Jet had appeared behind us with Melanie. 'Heard you had been rumbled. Never mind. It's probably best he knows that your main interests are flipping burgers and getting into concerts.'

'Better than designer clothes and footballers,' Rani snapped. 'You haven't a clue about going green, Jet.'

'Oh really? Is that so? Well, we shall just wait and see who River thinks is the greenest by the end of his time here.'

'You can't think it's going to be you, can you?'

'Well, you don't think it's going to be *you* after what just happened?'

'You couldn't care less about the planet!'

'Whatever. And I'm going to make Mr Trent think we do care, at least a whole lot more than you do.'

'Yes, but we're going to put it right with him.'

'Yeah right. We'll see, shall we?'

'We certainly will!' Rani snorted.

The gauntlet had been thrown down. This was war.

Then Mr Trent reappeared to check up on our cleaning up.

Jet saw him and said loudly in a fake-shocked tone, 'Don't tell me you had a *burger bar*?' She pulled a disgusted face and screwed up her nose. 'The smell! What were you thinking!

We're just on our way to enjoy some fresh air by the playing fields . . .'

Mr Trent gave her an approving smile and she skipped off.

I feel awful. Chloe and Rani are so upset. Maybe I have been selfish and greedy. I would like Dr Jennings to say 'No, no,' at this point, 'you have been clever and fulfilling a need in the community for decent burgers at lunch-time.' However, I know this isn't really true.

The front door has just banged downstairs. A feeling of impending doom has come upon me.

8.10 p.m.

An unpleasant talk with Mum followed by a tense meal. It is hard to enjoy your chicken stir-fry when your mum is saying, 'But what *were* you thinking?' every five seconds. And 'Selling burgers! In the changing room! Have you lost your *mind*?!' (Actually not very nice to mentally ill people to say that – but I decided not to mention it just then.) I don't know why Mr Trent had to go and tell her anyway. So he is a vegetarian, well, you would have thought that that would have made him more sensitive and caring as a person, wouldn't you? Hah!

We have a lunch-time detention on Friday and I feel for the others who will have that on top of not being considered beautiful spirits any more. But however much I protested he wouldn't let me take all the blame. And I deserve it all. It was my idea.

To make it up to Rani and Chloe, I am going to make a huge effort to show Mr T that we are not selfish capitalists, but caring Green Goddesses who know about saving energy and suchlike. I am going to start thinking about it now.

I will start by saving energy and switching off the radio. The LA Alphas are on and it's frankly too painful to listen to anyway.

RANI'S TIP: •

When life is very stressful, here's a stress-busting tip: try to breathe very slowly and concentrate on your breathing. If you are about to go into a scary situation, say to yourself on every 'out' breath, 'I am calm', or 'All is well'.

Chapter 7

Weird day in school.

Distinct absence of make-up on the faces of 9M this morning – even Jet and Melanie – which was quite a shock as no one has seen their natural skin colour since Year Six. Actually they still hadn't, due to Jet's orange hue. She does love her fake tan.

Rani and Chloe were barefaced as well. And no! Could it be true? Rani had her hair in plaits. I told her she looked like Pocahontas. She was genuinely thrilled. It's a worry. I know Rani in full-blown crush mode and she was showing all the signs. Still, looking at Chloe and around the rest of classroom, she was not alone.

Mrs McGuy's laser gaze took it all in, sweeping around the classroom and ending up on the manly form of Mr T, who had just come in the door. Her nostrils did a quick flare. Mrs McG isn't the sort of woman who is much impressed by a ponytail on a man. She sniffed and went to write notices on the board, leaving him to hand out our Devon lists. Everyone scanned them quickly.

Jet put up her hand. 'River?'

RIVER? *River!* You could see the back of Mrs McGuy's head stiffen. She whipped round from the board. She stared hard at Mr Trent.

'Yes, Jet?' he responded with a friendly smile. 'What is it?'

But we never got to hear what it was because he was interrupted by Mrs McGuy two inches from his face saying, 'MR TRENT. A word please. Outside.'

Zack looked up. 'Got a feeling River's gentle flowing waters are about to be stopped by a great big Mrs-McGuy-sized dam.'

And sure enough when they came back in, he looked rather flushed and cleared his throat and said that, as it was SCHOOL POLICY, we would have to call him Mr Trent from now on.

Schools are not democratic. They are dictatorships. With the head as supreme controller. However, I suppose I was struggling with the River thing anyway.

Mr Trent carried on talking. 'You'll need sleeping bags; we'll be in bunks in chalets in the grounds, which is a shame because I had hoped that we would be sleeping under canvas. There is nothing like sleeping in the great outdoors, feeling at one with nature. Have any of you lived under canvas? The kids at Rainbow Ridge would often just take themselves off into the wilderness for a few days. You really should try it . . . get close to the earth.'

Mrs McGuy's nostrils did another flare.

Jet's hand shot up. Not again. The closest she's been to the earth is a mud face pack.

'Yes, Jet, have you spent time under canvas?'

Jet coughed and gave Rani a meaningful look. 'Well, um, it's not so much where I've been, but where I *will be* this weekend. I'm going to be *going* camping.'

'Yeah right.' Zack laughed. 'I'll be careful not to trip over the guy ropes in New Look this Saturday.'

Jet gave him a withering sneer and went on.

'I just thought it would be good preparation as well, you know, for spending all that time, um . . . outside.'

'Excellent, Jet.' Mr T beamed. 'So great to hear that some of you are doing something interesting this weekend.'

'We're going camping too.'

Who said that?

My head span round.

'Yes,' Rani continued. 'Chloe and Carrie and me, we're going to be camping as well. We've been planning it for ages.'

What! Had she lost her mind?

'And we're going to be eating organic veggie food.'

'Well, that's just great, Rani. I think I must have underestimated this class. You must let us all know how you get on. Keep a note of any birds and animals you see and look around for ways to improve your environment. Fantastic. Well done, you girls. Are you looking forward to it, Carrie?' he asked.

I felt paralysed for a moment and then, looking at Rani, I knew what I had to do. I nodded dumbly. Rani and Chloe visibly relaxed. Mrs McGuy looked like someone had hit her over the head with a hammer.

'Might that not have been a rather rash thing to say,' I ventured at the lunch table (burger-less naturally). We were eating fast as we had to go up to detention.

'No. Because then he'll think we're cool and eco-friendly and love the planet and everything,' Rani gushed.

Chloe nodded. 'He is a bit of a hero, you know. He once lived in a tree to try and save a wood from a new road. You don't want him to think that we're bimbos or something, do you?' And she gave me a steady look. 'Not any more than he does already. After *yesterday* . . .'

'Mmm,' Rani added. 'And where are we going now? Oh yes, it's detention, isn't it, Carrie?'

Which was shameless blackmail on their part, but they were

right, I did not want Mr Trent to think badly of them. If it was going to help to make things up to them it would be worth it. And if it meant one little night under canvas so be it. I mean, how hard could it be? I've been in a caravan with my family in France. It's no big deal.

Maddy arrived at the table.

'Do you want to come on the camping trip, Maddy? I was thinking tomorrow night?' Rani enquired.

'I'd love to, but there's something I really want to see on Saturday on TV. I don't want to miss it.'

'Wow, Maddy, you're turning into a real goggle box addict these days, aren't you?' Chloe grinned. 'What *would* the kids at Rainbow Ridge say?'

Maddy blushed. 'I'm not! Really. Any other night would be OK. It's just I had made these plans . . .'

'You don't have to explain,' I sighed. 'Some people just aren't cut out to be eco-warriors and enjoy being at one with nature . . .'

'I love it!' Maddy defended herself stoutly. 'In America I went out camping in the wilderness all the time with my parents. I even saw a bear once. Anyway, where are you going? Any chance of bears there?'

'Doubt it.' Rani smiled.

'Why?' I asked. 'Where *are* we going?'

'Carrie's back garden.'

'What!'

'Got to be. Chloe doesn't have one and if we have it at mine my dad will insist on standing guard outside all night with a base-ball bat. It won't be relaxing, stuck in a tent with him silhouetted outside, poised to fight off sex-mad Boughton boys . . .'

'So you do have a tent at least?'

'Well, that's another thing . . .'

'You're joking? You don't even have a tent, Rani?'

'I thought you might have one.'

I was still spluttering when I spotted Nathan sitting down at the next table with Zack and Connor. Camping in my garden would have to wait. The rumours that Chris was up to his old tricks again were getting stronger, though Jennifer was doggedly refusing to believe them. If Chris actually was brave enough to end it himself, she might be single soon. I needed to move quickly in case Nathan thought of making a very poor decision.

I cleared my throat. 'Hem, I'm just going to pop over and say "Hi" to Nathan.' No one took any notice. 'Do you want to come with me, Maddy?'

She looked up from her shepherd's pie in surprise. 'I've only just sat down! And I have just seen him five minutes ago. I want to eat this before detention.'

'Thought I hadn't spoken to him, you know, properly, for a while . . . thought it might be nice to be friendly.'

Chloe did a double take. 'What *are* you on about, Carrie?'

'Going to say hi to Nathan. What's wrong with that? Just being nice.'

'You see him every single day, Carrie. What's this about? Oh no! Carrie? This isn't part of A PLAN, is it? You absolutely promised.' She gave me a warning glare.

'What plan?' Maddy queried.

'NO PLAN,' I hissed loudly at Chloe. What was she trying to do? Ruin everything?

I wanted to abandon talking to Nathan now Maddy wasn't

going to come with me, but I had got up by then and was standing awkwardly by the table.

'Well go on, then,' Rani said, giggling.

'Yes,' Chloe urged. 'Go on then. If you're so keen to have a chat with Nathan.'

'Actually I think it's nice you're being so friendly, I really do,' Rani said in a mock serious tone. 'We're not friendly enough with the boys in our own year, are we, Chloe?'

'No, Rani, we're not. Off you toddle, Carrie.'

Maddy was looking at the three of us as if we were totally mad.

'All right. I will.'

'Go on then.'

So I had no choice but to go over and I said a feeble 'Hi' and they all looked up and said 'Hi' in a curious but not unfriendly way.

They looked at me expectantly. I broke the silence. 'Er . . . how's it going?'

Nathan's brow furrowed. 'Fine. Since five minutes ago when we last saw you.'

There was a slightly awkward silence. Zack filled it.

'We were just wondering if there could possibly be a connection between River saying he liked women to look "natural" and the lack of slap on the girls' faces this morning? Coincidence, Carrie? Or not? Discuss.'

'Hmm,' I mused. 'The competition for Most Beautiful Spirit is definitely on. But it's not just for girls, you know – when are we going to see you lot express your inner —' But I didn't get a chance to finish because the next thing I knew I was being shoved aside by Jet. Gemma Brown was standing nervously at her side. Which was odd because Jet and Gemma do not hang out together. They have never hung out together. Gemma isn't exactly unpopular, but she doesn't have a best friends' group or anything like that. She has straight mousey hair, and sharp little features in a pale oval face. I would have thought that she was too quiet for Jet. However, when it comes to being the first in a queue or grabbing the best of anything that's being given out, I've noticed Gemma's not above digging a sneaky elbow in your side to get it before anyone else. Maybe it's that side of her personality which is the reason that we've never been big friends.

'Hi, Nathan,' Jet said in her foghorn voice.

Nathan started. 'Er, hello?'

Jet pushed Gemma forward. 'Hi, Nathan.' Gemma's pale blue eyes were riveted on him.

'Nathan! You changed your aftershave this morning or something?' Zack grinned.

Jet blasted on. 'I was thinking about the project. Thinking about teaming up. You guys should come down to the Coffee Bean sometime. Gemma's got some great ideas.'

I stared hard at her. What the hell was going on?

Jet continued, 'Thought it would be good to have you two creative types working side by side on our team.'

And then I got it.

She was poaching my starter boyfriend! For Gemma. Well, let's face it, it wasn't going to be for her or Melanie . . . I'm not a girl to cast doubts upon anyone's reputation, but it had to be said that their starter boyfriend days were in the *very* dim and distant past. Why on earth would she want Gemma to go out with Nathan? What's in it for her?

'Yes, you should come along one day,' I said lamely.

Jet's eyes narrowed. She gave me a level look. 'Where's Jack these days, Carrie?'

'Oh he's around, why?'

'Just wondered, that's all.' Her eyes swivelled meaningfully in Nathan's direction. 'Thought you'd be too busy going out with Jack and going on camping trips to have much time for any extra social life.'

'Not at all, you're never too busy to have time for friends, are you?'

'No. Never too busy. So you'll come to the Coffee Bean, Nathan?' It was more of an order from Jet than a request.

Nathan stared desperately at the other boys.

'He might,' Zack said finally. 'But you're weirding the boy out with all the attention. What with that and the no make-up thing. What happened to the real Jet? Is she orbiting earth in your mother ship?'

Jet gave him her best crushing look.

Connor frowned. 'This has nothing to do with Nathan's dad's new job, has it?'

'What? What are you talking about? What a random thing to say.' She laughed nervously.

'You know, Nathan's dad —'

'I have no idea what you're talking about . . .'

Zack grinned. 'I hope you never want a career in acting, Jet. I bet this is something to do with —' But Jet had grabbed Gemma's arm and was dragging her off across the dining hall.

'. . . the fact that his dad has just been appointed the physiotherapist at Middleton United.' He finished to the empty space where they had stood.

I scooted quickly back to Chloe, Rani and Maddy.

'What the hell was that all about?' Rani asked. 'Spill.'

But I didn't want to say anything in front of Maddy. She didn't need to know she had a rival. And Jet and Melanie were backing that rival. I realised the task ahead may be more complicated than I had imagined.

'It was about nothing really, just being friendly. Did you know that Nathan's dad is the new physio at Middleton United?'

Rani looked at me as if I'd lost my mind. 'Yes, and?'

'Nothing, just that Jet is very keen to be in with him now.'

'Well, she'll have to find a very clever way in; she's ignored him for years, why should he do her any favours? It's not like she's his girlfriend or anything.'

No, I thought, as we trooped off to the detention room, but she's aiming to be his girlfriend's best mate.

I'm going to go downstairs now to ask:

1. *Can we camp in the garden?*
2. *Do we have a tent?*

I have also been researching natural beauty remedies that we can find outdoors. I will ask Mum before I raid her herb pots. Relationships are still fragile after the burger incident, but I am hoping this might show I am moving in a new direction. Also she has taken all my money as repayment and let's just say most of my beauty products will be home-grown for the foreseeable future.

CHLOE'S TIP: • • • • • • • • • • • • • • • • •

The girls at Rainbow Ridge didn't have wonderful skin from eating chips and pizza. They drank loads of water and ate lots of fruit and vegetables. This is even more important if you live in a polluted city. Eating lots of fresh fruit and veggies helps your body fight the damage from pollution.

Chapter 8

Eating toast in bed, waiting for Rani and Chloe to come over.

Spoke to Mum and Dad about the camping last night. Unfortunately Ned was present. He's hyper because this casting agent is coming to Year Seven to look at possible people for a project; nobody seems to know if it's TV or film yet.

His reaction was typical. 'You! Camping! That's a joke. Will the extension lead on your hairdryer reach as far as the garden?'

'Ha di ha, Ned. Excuse me while I split my sides. We are going to commune with nature. We can, can't we, Dad?'

'Course you can, Carrie. I think that's a great idea. Your mum and I used to go camping when we first met. And don't you worry about a tent. I'll get the old one we used to use out of the attic. We loved it, didn't we?'

Mum smiled, but I noticed she didn't actually reply.

Dad got up to search the attic, but when he got to the kitchen door he turned around. 'I've got a great idea. Why don't I camp out with you? I could get out the little one-man tent that Max took on his Duke of Edinburgh trip. Tell some spooky stories, toast some marshmallows.' And then he disappeared up the stairs. Mum went to get some parsley from the garden.

Ned leaned back on his chair and started singing 'Kumbaya' and strumming an imaginary guitar. I told him to shut up.

'Just practising, Carrie,' he responded. 'You know – for when it's Dad, and your mates all sitting round the fire, Dad on the old guitar trying to pick out one of his old hippie songs and telling them about the camping trips of his youth. He's bound to wear those slightly too tight shorts too . . .'

1.30 p.m.

Rani and Chloe arrived nice and early. Thought they were acting a bit shifty, but due to the Dad crisis, I didn't notice the bag till later.

They thought his idea was funny in that hysterical way you do when it's not *your* dad. Even though my dad is a lovely man, camping out in the garden with my friends and me was about the most horrendous thing I could possibly imagine. I felt quite faint.

'You will just have to be tactful and tell him that it's a girls' only night. Nettle face packs, etc. He'll understand,' Chloe soothed.

He took it well. But you do wonder what goes on in their heads sometimes. I was only just in time; he was coming down the ladder from the attic again and he had his old guitar over his shoulder.

When I came back into my room Chloe had started taking things out of her bag: T-shirts, long cotton neckscarves, string and dye.

'Not in a trillion million years,' I said.

'Come on . . .' Rani pleaded.

'Not if I were the only girl in the world, in the universe. Not if every other person in the whole wide world, no, the whole galaxy were blind . . .'

'But Carrie, it will be cool. Tie-dye is cool.'

'Why can't you two do it and leave me out of it?'

'Because it will look weird if you don't look the same.'

'Exactly, instead of you and Chloe looking like you've lost all sense of style and taste, I will too.'

'We think we'll look great.'

Rani looked serious. She bit her lip bravely. 'OK, don't do it. I simply thought you might want to support me the way I supported *you*. It was a pain having to miss a lunch hour sitting in detention yesterday, wasn't it? I don't think I heard myself complain, but if you don't want to . . .'

'Oh God! OK. OK. How much longer is this debt going to take to pay off?'

'You are a star, Carrie. I know this will impress him loads. We will look so Rainbow Ridge.'

Out of my window I can see Rani and Chloe lying in the garden. On the washing line three T-shirts and three large cotton squares are drying fast in the sunshine. I am going with Mum to the health food shop now to buy the scrummy organic food for this evening. When I say I'm going to help my friends, I do it wholeheartedly. Mum offered to cook a big veggie chilli for us, but I said no thank you, I will be doing all the cooking myself. Have to admit to a secret desire to impress Jack and get some respect back after his disapproval over the Boughton Burgers thing. Dad got out the camping gas stove and I have given Mum my new food list. Mr T mentioned alfalfa sprouts as being very good for you. And mung beans. I'm not sure I've ever seen a mung bean before, but they can't be that hard to cook. I do baked beans all the time.

Our camping agenda is as follows:

1. Boys come round and help us put up Dad's tent.
2. Collect twigs and sticks to make fire for cooking delicious meal.
3. Make totally delicious meal and impress Jack with my organisation and wide-ranging culinary skills. Therefore proving I am not a shallow, materialistic person.
4. After delicious meal and Jack is suitably impressed, make tasty, hot herbal brew.
5. Eat chocolate with it and sit around making up lyrics for song to impress Mr Trent (Rani's idea).
6. Dad will come out about nine forty-five p.m. and stand around awkwardly. Mum will be watching from the kitchen window to see how he's doing. The boys will take the hint and leave.
7. Natural beauty treatment time. Face packs, hair rinses, etc. Only using water from outside tap. Can warm it up a bit on roaring fire.
8. Eat biscuits.
9. Lie under stars contemplating the mysteries of the universe.

I think Mr Trent will approve and I will have paid my debt to Rani and Chloe at last. Anyway, it will all be worth it to be so much more green than Jet. I can't believe her feeble plans for camping will be anything like as impressive as that little lot. Even if it is in our back garden. I hope Rani and Chloe appreciate my efforts to help them reach adequate spiritual beauty.

5.00 p.m.

Back from food shop. The strange variety of food available in a health food shop! Who knew?

Looking out of the window I can see Jack and Tom in the garden now, spreading out all the tent bits before putting it up.

Kenny is laying out guy ropes. Dad's tent turned out to be from the dark ages and has lots of parts to it. Strange bits of canvas and rope are taking up an awful lot of garden. Rani and Chloe are collecting twigs and sticks for the fire. Later we will gather mint, parsley and cucumber. We have decided to stick to our plan and reject the gas stove as it saps the earth's resources – why would we use it, when we can make our own roaring fire from sticks and twigs? I have come up to my room to find hairgrips to hold the entrance to the tent together – apparently the zip is broken. It doesn't matter really. It's so hot and sticky today anyway. It is going to be great. I can feel myself bonding with the universe already.

7.00 p.m.

In my room not sneaking a quick break, but getting a tent up is a lot harder than it looks. Even with all of us working at it, it took forever. But at last it is up. There is just enough room inside for three sleeping bags laid out side-by-side and our provisions.

I went over them with Rani.

'One large bar of chocolate, organic.'

'Check,' Rani answered.

'One plate of mung beans.'

Rani proffered a plate of likely looking sprouty things.

'Think that's them. One bag alfalfa sprouts.'

'Check. Carrie, what are you actually thinking of cooking with those?'

'We are having a bean stew with mung beans and alfalfa sprout salad.'

'Yum, sounds delicious.'

'Three cans of kidney beans and a bag of quinoa.'

'What?'

'Quinoa, pronounced "keen-wah", very nutritious. Sort of porridgy. I read you can add it to stews.'

'Mmm, OK.'

'That's it then. Oh and the herbal tea.'

'Mmm. It looks suitably, er, grassy.'

'Well, it would do. It's herbs, isn't it? I thought we could add parsley to it.'

The real reason that I am back up here in my room again is that I have come to collect some pens and paper from my school bag for writing beautiful poems about the natural world. I found a half finished packet of Maltesers at the bottom. I can see from the window that the neighbours are setting up their barbecue. I hope they are not going to be too noisy. Rani and Chloe will not want the tranquil nature of the evening to be spoiled.

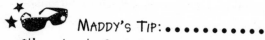 MADDY'S TIP: •

It's not only for hot summer days, but every day: wear sunscreen. Don't just wear it for sunbathing, but when putting up tents, shopping, walking round town and just hanging around out of doors. You can buy moisturisers with them built in now so there's no excuse. You don't see the damage not wearing it does now, but you will when you get older. Get with the programme. Never leave home without it.

Chapter 9

Sunday 7.45 a.m.

It's hard to know where to begin really.

Let's just say I will be doing things differently if I do it again.

Which, frankly, doesn't seem likely. There is only so much a girl can stand.

I can see that Rani and Chloe are still fast asleep. I'm not surprised. I would be too if I could. But the events of last night keep galloping around my brain. What could we have done to make it less of a disaster? I have made a list.

1. Don't let boys put up a tent made a hundred years ago.
2. When your dad offers to help, let him.
3. The number of twigs and sticks Rani and Chloe can forage for in the average back garden does not equal the amount needed to make a decent fire. They said they tried their best, but honestly . . . don't get stranded with them anywhere chilly. Or anywhere you might want to eat anything served above a tepid temperature.
4. Kidney and mung bean stew, with quinoa, needs to be served piping hot. In fact, I would go so far as to say that if you are trying to impress your friends with your culinary skills, quinoa, mung and kidney bean stew is not the dish to do it with.
5. Appreciate that herbal tea can be wincingly bitter. Adding parsley does not help.
6. Do not eat the chocolate and biscuits within ten minutes of everyone arriving. Even though it may seem like a good idea at the

time, later on in the evening, staring into a cup of warm water and grass, you will feel very differently.

7. *Don't schedule a quiet evening communing with nature and writing on a day your neighbours are having a barbecue. With a disco.*

It turned the songwriting part of the evening into a complete fiasco. For example, Tom's contribution:

'The daisies lift their tiny heads from grassy floor
Take That is belting out from right next door.'

And Jack's:

'The sun burns down, the painted gate it blisters,
Hooray! I hear the Scissor Sisters.'

You see it wasn't at all satisfactory, and then Rani tried to save the situation and said that Mr Trent wanted us to make notes about birds and wildlife too. Kenny immediately offered,

'The Robin in the hedgerow sits,
I think Madonna's got great . . .'

Hey ho. It was at that point I put my pen and paper to one side and abandoned the idea.

Finally, check the weather forecast. The first drops of rain had begun to plop down after the boys had gone home. The sky soon became dark with bulging thunder clouds. A huge rumble sounded the death knell of the disco. So you see, it wasn't all bad.

Rani, Chloe and I got into the tent and started on our natural beauty therapies to cheer ourselves up. I mixed up some yogurt and cucumber and Chloe mashed a banana into some honey. Rani was working on a parsley and mint face freshener. She had the plants in a saucepan and was pounding them with a wooden spoon.

'Rani! You're supposed to be "preparing the herbs for infusion" not fighting off a vicious attack,' Chloe said, frowning.

The rain got worse and starting coming in through the gaps between hairgrips and a hole above our heads. Rani went out to put her anorak over the outer sheet. This worked for a while, but then a little rivulet got going. It ran from the tear down the inside of the tent and pooled under my sleeping bag. I moved it, but the water seemed to chase the bag around its little bit of tent so I abandoned trying to rescue it.

We put on our face-masks and Rani bravely went out to get some water for her face rinse from the garden tap. You were supposed to add the herbs to boiling water but, due to the lack of fire, this bit had been abandoned.

'How will we wash this off?' Chloe frowned as she patted the last of the banana on her chin.

Other leaks had begun in the tent. They were merging with the puddle (now lake) in the middle of the floor.

I turned my head to listen to the drumming rain on the canvas.

'Are you kidding?'

Rani returned looking pleased with herself. It was apparent she had simply filled the pan with water and then tipped everything over her head. A sprig of parsley rested over one eye and tendrils of wet mint were woven into her bedraggled locks. A kind person would say it looked mermaidy.

'Go away! You're dripping everywhere!' I screeched.

She lifted her foot out of a puddle on the tent floor. 'Does it really matter any more?'

Chloe and I looked at each other's pale, sticky faces.

'No,' we said in unison.

'Well, come outside and dance in the rain with me. It's fantastic.'

So we did. We ran outside and then round and round the garden, shouting mad things and swirling and twirling in the thunder and lightning. Now that is what I call appreciating nature. Our neighbour, Mrs Read, came to the fence under a huge golf umbrella and offered us a tray of sausages. So we said thank you, thank you and took one in each hand and ate them as we danced. And it was all most spiritual.

Then two things happened. Firstly, I was chanting something stupid, waving sausages and walking backwards and I keeled over into the wheelbarrow, which was full of grass clippings. Secondly, as I lay giggling, covered in the remains of a pot of yogurt, a ton of wet grass clippings and some half-eaten sausages, I saw two figures standing frozen in the kitchen doorway. I looked to each side of me and saw that Rani and Chloe had seen them too. One was Mum and the other . . . Well, well, well. It was Mr Trent.

Dad has brought me tea. That is kind. I expect he will make one for Mum too. I hope she appreciates it. It'll be a long time before she gets one from me.

Chloe is waking up at last. All our sleeping bags are sodden, cold and bloated with water. Luckily, they are draped over the radiators in the hall. Chloe and Rani are cosily curled up in a bed of duvets on my bedroom floor. Mum said one of them could sleep in Max's room, but we didn't want to totally lose the 'camping' feel. We lasted in the tent till Rani had a brief gap in being hysterical about Mr Trent's surprise appearance and got a giggling fit about something I'd said earlier. I don't know if it was her giggle-vibrations, but at that point, her side of the tent collapsed. Quickly followed by my side. From the middle of the tent, under a pile of wet canvas came a muffled voice. 'We must do this again sometime,' Chloe sighed.

They are waking up now. I hope they can still see there is a funny side this morning.

11.00 a.m.

Rani and Chloe have left. Not really seeing the funny side. We are meeting up in the Coffee Bean later this afternoon.

I am barely speaking to Mum. Yesterday evening (OK, even though it *was* in a damp, disgusting-food way) I *was* managing to make up for the burger business crisis with them. It may not have been quite as we imagined, but our version of it at school tomorrow would have been more impressive.

'We can't even lie to him,' Chloe wailed flinging herself on to her pillow to demonstrate her agony. 'He saw me, oh my God, he saw me with a face pack on.'

'*Yes* – but made of *natural* ingredients,' I reminded her. I was beginning to wish they hadn't woken up. She was not soothed.

'And with a sausage in each hand,' she groaned.

Rani, lying on her back in her duvet nest, raised a fist and shook it in the general direction of the window. 'Curse you, Carrie's next-door neighbour and your damnable sausage temptation. What really depresses me —'

'God, Rani, you told me what really depressed you about a thousand times last night. What about me? I was lying in a wheelbarrow covered with cucumber and grass cuttings. It's not nice you know, unexpectedly being caught looking like a salad.'

Rani took a deep breath and gave me a level stare. 'What really depresses *me*, is that I thought we had clawed back a bit of respect since the burger thing and now we are simply back to square one. He will never think that we are Green Goddesses now.'

'Indeed.' Chloe was also giving me a special look.

'It wasn't my fault! How was I to know that Mr Trent was going to come over and drop off the school trip risk assessment thingy for Mum to look at?'

Rani pursed her lips and was examining her nails.

'How could I have known? *She* didn't even know, he was just passing and thought he'd drop it in. It's not my fault he asked Mum where we were camping this weekend and she took him to the kitchen to show him, is it?'

Chloe sighed. 'S'pose not.'

'And I know it was unforgivable of her to let Mr Trent into the kitchen, but she asked how she was to know we'd be dancing around with sprigs of parsley up our noses and waving sausages?'

'I suppose it *would* be hard to predict that *particular* scenario.' Chloe nodded. 'You're right. It isn't your fault.'

'It's true, Chloe, it isn't Carrie's fault.' Rani sat up. 'This camping trip was my idea, anyway. I'm not being fair blaming you. Not fair at all. It's just that . . . that I feel he may have got the impression that we were, um . . . on the immature side, the not quite taking it all seriously side. Your mum said he left immediately with barely a word. And I can't bear the thought of him thinking badly of us again.'

'It was a pretty striking impression,' Chloe sighed again. 'But we were *kind* of being green. You did have a pile of parsley on your head, Rani, and we were dancing around like water spirits.'

'Oh it was "Green" all right,' I said, 'but I'm thinking it did rather fall down on the "Goddess" part.'

I got out of bed and put on my fluffy pink dressing gown.

'Come on, let's get dressed. Let's go downstairs and have an enormous power breakfast. We are going to think of something to do to redeem this situation. And it will be marvellous. We will be his shining stars. We will make him see that, compared to Jet and Melanie and a little bit of camping, we are so green we are practically compost.'

Which made me wonder. How *did* Jet and Melanie get on last night?

 CARRIE'S TIP: • • • • • • • • • • • • • • • • • •

To make a parsley and mint freshener that actually works this is what Rani should have done:

You will need:

12g of fresh parsley

1 teaspoon of dried mint leaves (ask your mum if she has some in the spice rack) or a good handful of fresh mint, chopped up

225ml of boiling water (be very, very, careful)

Add the parsley and mint to the water and leave to infuse for thirty minutes. Strain the solution through a cloth and pour into a bottle. *Voilà!* Totally natural. (Preservative free, so don't keep it for more than three or four days.)

Chapter 10

Sunday 9.00 p.m.

We didn't have long to wait to find out the answer to *that* question.

It seems like a year since we had our power breakfast this morning.

We met up in the Coffee Bean as planned (after hours of homework – Mum *made* me, and after the night I'd had!). I couldn't help worrying that Jack wasn't going to have been as impressed by the evening as I had hoped. I sidled on to the seat next to him. Chloe, Tom and Rani sat opposite.

'Sorry about yesterday,' I murmured.

He gazed at me, puzzled. 'Sorry? What for?'

'What for? The food for a start . . .'

'The food!' Jack looked astonished. 'The food was extraordinary, unforgettable! In fact, if I really try . . .' He pushed his tongue around the inside of his mouth. '. . . I can still taste it now.'

I tried to pout, but couldn't help grinning. Jack always had the knack of making any situation all right. He put his arm around me and kissed my cheek. 'It was a great evening, Carrie, it really was.'

Maddy appeared and slid into the space on the other side of me.

'I'm sorry I missed it. I truly am. I would have given anything to see Mr Trent's expression.'

Rani's face clouded. 'Well, I can tell you it was pure shock and horror.'

'I think I detected a little bit of fear too,' I added. 'And Maddy we told *you*, but you must promise, promise, promise, like Tom and Jack have,' (Jack made a zippy motion across his mouth and looked saintly) 'not to tell another soul in our class about what happened. Promise?'

'Promise.'

'Hi, Carrie.' I looked up. It was Nathan. His face looked nervous. I looked around.

'You meeting Zack and Connor?'

'Supposed to be. We said we'd meet here around now. They'll show up in a minute.'

I saw my chance.

'Well hey! Why don't you drag up a chair and join us?'

He would be sitting right next to Maddy. I could see she was giving him a friendly smile. How lucky was this?

He bit his lip, 'I'd love to, but, er . . .'

'NATHAN!'

You'd recognise that foghorn blast anywhere.

'Jet,' he responded feebly.

She bounded up and scooped her arm through his. 'Come on, Nathan, Melanie and Gemma are waiting at our table and we've got a lot of work to get through.'

We all craned our necks to peer along the café and saw Melanie in full make-up, her dark hair scraped back to within an inch of its life into a high ponytail and her skirt would have made me a nice hairband. On her feet she was wearing a pair of high-heeled, white shiny sandals, very similar to the ones that Jet was wearing with her designer jeans, wide gold belt and huge gold earrings. The natural look was obviously only for school. Melanie gave us an icy wiggle of her red-taloned fingers. Sitting next to her was their new best friend, Gemma, dressed more simply in a blue cotton skirt, T-shirt and short black jacket. Her eyes were focused intently on Nathan.

'Can't we wait for Zack and Connor?' Nathan pleaded.

Jet's ferociously plucked eyebrows wrinkled. 'Don't be stupid.'

'Well, I'll go and get a drink then.' And he headed off for the counter.

Jet turned to look at us, paused and then gave a slow smile. 'Now then, goodness me, wasn't that a storm last night? All that *rain*. I really felt for you. You must have got totally soaked. Did you? Did you get totally soaked? You *poor* things . . .'

She stared down at our silent faces.

'Well, what happened? Don't you want to talk about it?'

'How did *your* camping trip go, Jet?' Rani interrupted. 'You and Melanie look very – how shall I put this – well-groomed, for people who slept out in a storm.'

She laughed raucously. 'You are kidding, aren't you? I wouldn't camp out for a million pounds.'

'But you told Mr Trent!'

'Yeah, yeah, whatever. But I was never going to actually *do* it. Camping is way too much of an effort and I needed a free evening to phone Nathan about a great idea I had last night. You know he's into this environment thing so I thought I'd ask him again, him being so kind and everything . . .' – she gave me a special smile – '. . . if we could think of something *together*. Melanie, Gemma, me and him.'

'Not just you, Nathan said Zack and Connor are coming too.'

Jet ignored this. 'And Nathan's ideas are really going to impress Mr Trent. Much better than camping in the soggy old rain.'

'And what is that great idea?' I asked.

Jet beamed. 'OK, you know he's so good at art, he's agreed to design a poster as part of my, oops, sorry, *our* new campaign.'

'And what is your new campaign?' Chloe asked.

'Against testing cosmetics on animals.'

There was a stunned silence.

'I didn't know that was a cause that you felt strongly about,' croaked Chloe.

Jet smoothed one of her virtually non-existent eyebrows and shrugged her shoulders. 'Whatever.'

'Well, Jet,' Jack said, grinning, 'the animal world will be eternally grateful. There must be laboratories all over the world where your make-up is manufactured, where, right this minute, fluffy bunnies are throwing little goodbye parties and packing their tiny bunny suitcases.'

Jet looked puzzled.

Rani leapt in before she could think about it further. 'That's a good idea, Jet. I see you and Melanie are both back in full warpaint now we are out of school and out of sight of Mr T. I take it it's all animal friendly.' (Rani: future vet speaking.) 'I hope no whales died to make that very striking shade of lippie . . .'

Jet's eyes opened wide. 'You what?! I haven't got a clue.'

'B – b – but your campaign?' Chloe stammered.

'Yeah? Well, that's for school and Mr Trent thinking we're great, isn't it? Not for real life for goodness' sake!'

Nathan was coming back to our table. Jet headed towards him, scooping him up as she drew level. 'Come on, let's get on with it!' she barked and marched him firmly back to where Melanie and Gemma were busy making room on their table.

'Poor boy. It's like a lamb to the slaughter,' Tom sighed.

'I know!' I cried. 'And he's much too nice to say, "I don't want to do this with you. Push off." They've just *steamrollered* him.'

'Zack and Connor should be along any minute and then he'll have back-up in case of attack.' Maddy grinned.

'Yes, but where are they?' I wailed. 'It's obvious Jet wants to get Gemma off with Nathan.'

'And we all know why . . .' Rani commented.

'Which makes him so much more vulnerable,' I whimpered.

'Vulnerable to what?' Maddy asked.

'Yeah? What's wrong with it?' Tom rubbed his thick dark brown hair.

'She's so not right for him,' I said primly.

'Why not, Carrie?' Jack asked, in a slightly dangerous tone.

'Gemma's so weirdly intense about everything. She looks all quiet and butter wouldn't melt in her mouth, but she's got a steely core.'

'A *steely core*! Jeez! Where the hell do you get that from?' Maddy gasped.

'From when we were designing the dresses with the French girls. Remember she was in a team with Tess? Before they stopped speaking to each other she went round to Tess's house a few times. She had this thing for Tess's brother, Baz. She was really pushy; Baz said she just wouldn't take no for an answer. He had to talk to her in a seriously tough way before she got the message. And you know what she's like at pushing to the front when anything's on offer. But with someone like Nathan, who hates hurting anyone's feelings . . . He couldn't be tough with anyone, and she knows it. It's his kind personality that has got him into this situation. I bet Jet told him that if he didn't help with their project he didn't care about animals or something . . .'

'How come you know all this, Carrie?' Jack asked.

'I know it because Tess told me at lunch the other day, when I first got an inkling about what Jet was up to. And it is for this reason *and no other*,' I said staring meaningfully into his eyes, 'I don't think it's a good idea.'

'She might not be interested.' Maddy shrugged.

'Oh she's interested,' I said looking over at the table where she sat next to Nathan. He glanced up and gave me a nervous smile.

'Why can't they just be friendly with Nathan themselves?' Chloe asked.

'Jet's cleverer than that. She's never shown the slightest interest in Nathan and anyway she knows Zack and Connor would see through her. But if she can get him together with Gemma, then she can have some influence over things.'

'How does that work?' Maddy asked.

'Because Gemma would owe her. Gemma would never have quite had the nerve to set up the project thing, or to ask Nathan out. But Jet never minds just barging in to get her own way and she's done the hard work for her.'

Jack was looking intently at me. 'Have you quite finished, Sherlock Holmes?'

I sat up as straight as I could. 'Yes I have.'

'And there's no other reason, at all, for not wanting Gemma to go out with Nathan?'

'None at all.'

Maddy frowned at him. 'What possible other reason could Carrie have for caring who Nathan goes out with, apart from thinking he's a nice guy and not wanting to see him hurt?'

'Indeed.' Jack nodded.

Rani and Chloe looked a bit shifty at this point and I was just getting worried that Maddy might pick up on this when we were interrupted.

'WELL, WE'LL BE OFF NOW!' Jet was passing our table, with Melanie scampering behind her.

Gemma was still at the table with Nathan.

'Where are Zack and Connor?' I asked again.

Jet clapped her hand over her mouth.

'OH MY GOD! I totally forgot. I phoned them just before we came out to say it wasn't on, you know, I wasn't feeling so good and I told them it was cancelled. And, oh dear, I completely forgot to tell them that it was back on. Felt better suddenly.'

'Well, it looks like Nathan's calling them now.' Chloe observed.

Jet's eyes flicked over to him and she smirked. 'So I see, but they live in Dursford, and it's going to take them at least half an hour to get here. I don't think they'll bother, as it's Sunday and the café closes at four-thirty. And oh look! It's nearly four o' clock now. Bye . . .'

And she swanned out of the Coffee Bean with Melanie behind her.

RANI'S TIP: •

If you are going for a 'look', like nautical for example, or ethnic peasant girl, or even designer label, it's best not to go over the top. One piece of clothing and an accessory will get the message across with style - chucking everything at it is the way of the fashion victim.

Chapter 11

On the bus.

'Yeah, she phoned last night. They are one hundred per cent going out now. She's dead excited about it. High as kite on *lurve* . . .'

Jet is behind us and I'm not exactly eavesdropping, but you can't ignore her voice. I noticed when I got on the bus that she and Melanie are back to the scrubbed-face natural look this morning.

I am glad Jet does not know that I write this diary on the bus sometimes. She would give me a hard time about it because she thinks diary writing like mine is from the olden days. Rani understands that I will need it to recall details when I'm having my therapy sessions with Dr Jennings. And it's much lighter than a laptop (if only I had one). I have put a new cover over the Little Mermaid picture on the front and have written, *Homework Notes*, in big letters on it. Now I hope she just thinks I'm a bit nerdy.

'High as a kite on *lurve*! That's brilliant,' Melanie cooed. 'You know what this means?'

'I KNOW!'

I know what it means. It means Nathan has been nabbed. That is very bad news indeed.

Rani. Please do not poke me with your pink pencil with the little doggie on the end. I am insulted to be attacked with something so girlie and tacky.

Rani, I *do* like animals. I like them a lot. Just because I'm not obsessed like some people and don't sleep with six old teddy bears and go hoppity skip around my bedroom with all my woodland pals over jumps I made by propping all my books up.

Yeah, you say that was a long time ago and you are laughing, but I wonder is that the laughter of someone trying to cover up the hideous truth?

Rani has just told me that the truly green do not waste time worrying about people's love lives. They get on with the job of trying to help the environment and do not let themselves get distracted.

Maddy has just distracted us by leaning over and saying, 'I need to talk to you two about something important.'

We both looked at her curiously.

'It's this. You know I'm going to Los Angeles this summer.'

'Yes and we couldn't be more jealous, though actually I'm going to India to see my gran and that's pretty cool,' Rani replied.

'Well, my parents have said that I can take a friend. They would pay all expenses.'

We both looked at her open-mouthed. We'd seen pictures of Maddy's house in LA and it is A-MAZING. Pool and everything.

'So . . .' She took a deep breath. 'You know I'd like to take all of you, but it has to be just one and so I thought I'd ask you two if you minded if I took Chloe. It's just that I know she doesn't really do much in the summer . . .'

'Maddy,' I said after a brief pause to take it all in, 'I think that is the most sensational idea I have heard in a very long time.'

Rani said, 'Hear, hear!'

And it is. And I am truly glad for Chloe.

I asked Rani, 'Do you think Nathan *really* asked Gemma out?'
Put that pencil away.

6.30 p.m.

Am having a cup of tea in my room. And a chocolate digestive or six. It has been a very strange day.

We met Chloe going into school and Maddy asked her about LA and she went bonkers and Maddy's mum is going to phone her mum to discuss arrangements. I am pleased for her, but now Rani isn't looking over my shoulder I do have to say that I wish, wish, wish it was me. Of course it has to be Chloe, I understand that, but LA! It would have to be the most exciting holiday ever. No long drive to France sitting with Ned in the back of the car. Chloe's brother, Jim, will miss *her* though. He is very preoccupied with the battery hens issue at his school at the moment. The school has been offered some hens rescued from a battery farm. A chance for an outdoor life pecking around the school grounds instead of stuffed in a wire cage. The hens cost virtually nothing, but the school can't afford the henhouse and you have to have one to lock them in at night to keep them safe from foxes. Jim is very worried about them so I hope hearing Chloe's going away won't add to his troubles. My family have not booked the French mobile home yet. Mum and Dad want to wait to see if Ned gets this audition thing and then we'll 'work round it'. But actually I'm cool with this, as it will give me more time with Jack.

First person we met at the lockers was Gemma.

'Hi!' she gushed, eyes bright. 'Just wanted you to know that Nathan and I are an item now, just letting everyone know.'

'Well, er, that's great,' Chloe congratulated. 'You seem very, um, pleased.'

Gemma hugged her school bag. 'Oh I am! He's so nice. We get on so well and have so much in common . . . Must dash, everyone will want to hear all the details!' And she sped off.

'Nice to see love blooming.' Jennifer had appeared.

'Actually, to be honest, Jennifer, we always thought that you were the only girl that Nathan was interested in.'

'Chloe, I know he likes me, but why would I be interested in him when I have Chris? In spite of other girls making a play for him. I hope you do not believe the stupid rumours. He's told me they are just spread by jealous girls who want him for themselves,' she said, looking daggers at me.

'Is it just girls who are delusional? Or do you think boys are this mad too?' Rani asked a few minutes later on the way up to the form room.

'Both I think. Desperation to be loved or to simply have a boyfriend can make people refuse to believe the obvious facts in front of them.'

'You're talking about my ancient crush on Jonny Poynton, aren't you, Carrie?'

'I'm not! I'm just making an observation.'

'Then I thought I should go out with Kenny because you all had boyfriends. Thank goodness you helped me come to my senses and I realised it doesn't matter one diddley-i-doh. I can't believe I was so dumb.'

'Well, what about Danny and me!' I said. 'I pined in my room for days believing it was the end of the world and *he* kissed like a vacuum cleaner!'

'But you did accept it was over, Carrie,' Chloe observed. 'You didn't believe there was still a relationship when there wasn't.'

'He was living in Birmingham.'

'You know what I mean.'

I stopped in the corridor. 'Let's make a pact.'

'What about?' Chloe and Rani asked.

'That we will *never, ever, ever* let each other get delusional and lose all sight of reality over a boy . . .'

'Pact. And what will be the signal that will bring us back to our senses?'

Rani made a jabbing motion in the air. 'I've got my pointy pink pencil.'

8.25 p.m.

I have been downstairs to hear the news from Mum that the casting agent has been in. She watched a drama and music lesson. She said she seemed nice and Ned said she came over to chat with him at the end. She's going to phone the school if she thinks anyone might be right for the part. I asked Mum what it was for and she said some school programme. Which is disappointing.

What is also disappointing is that Maddy is no further forward in the boyfriend stakes. I know no one *needs* a boyfriend. Look at Rani and loads of girls in our class. It's just an instinctive feeling I have that Maddy *would* like one. Not that she's said or done anything to say she would, but I'm seldom wrong when it comes to my intuition on these things.

Gemma on the other hand has set off at a flying pace.

'GEMMA STEVENS! Who gave you permission to move desks?'

Mrs McGuy's beams were burning. Gemma had swapped desks with Cara and she was now nestled next to a very embarrassed-looking Nathan.

'Cara doesn't mind, I asked her,' chirped Gemma. Ooooh dear. Big mistake. I could see Mrs McG taking a deep breath; she placed both hands firmly on her desk and leaned forward.

'Reeeally? *Cara* doesn't mind? Well, that's all right then. As long as *Cara* doesn't mind, but there is one small problem, Gemma.'

Gemma looked curious.

'I MIND! Move your desks back to where you were *immediately.*'

Gemma looked mutinous, but no one remotely sane is going to fight the wrath of Mrs McG so she and Cara started dragging their desks back. I noticed Nathan kept his eyes straight ahead, ignoring Gemma's tragic looks in his direction. Made resolve to talk to Zack and Connor at lunch about what's going on there.

Double geog. Seemed every girl in 9M has got a scheme going to save energy or whales or orang-utans or something. Everyone was clamouring to shout out about theirs until Mr T put up his hands to protect himself from the onslaught.

'Hey! You guys! It's like, you know, one at a time here. It's cool that you have all been thinking so hard about this, but I can't hear if you all talk at me at once. Let's start with Jet's group.'

Jet brandished the poster that Nathan had done. It was good. It was a black and white Andy-Warhol-type photo of a kitten. Over the top Nathan had super-imposed garish, grotesque make-up in vivid blues, pinks and scarlet. Underneath, as if scrawled in lipstick, *Don't be a sight for sore eyes.*

Mr T nodded gravely. 'Good, who did that poster? Nathan? Good work, man, good work. The other thing to think about now is packaging of make-up. Do you need an energy consuming black plastic case and mirror with every small amount of powder? Some firms now use recyclable packaging; it's worth trying to find out who they are.'

Jet nodded. As if her bag wasn't clattering with twenty plastic compacts, eyeshadow holders, bottles and jars.

Chloe, Rani, Maddy and I then explained our idea. In our school, paper, plastic and glass is already recycled. They go into separate bins. But shoes and clothes can be recycled too. We thought we'd host a big 'Reusing Awareness Day' next term; make posters, information sheets, etc. We'd have yummy healthy things to eat and drink, etc. along with a big second-hand clothes sale. Everyone could bring in their unwanted things and they could swap or sell them. All proceeds to an environmental charity. I'd asked Mum and she said she thought it was a great idea. And so did Mr Trent. Chloe and Rani's beautiful spirits were back in the race. And in spite of the fact he thinks flowers in the wind are nature's disco, I feel quite good about it too.

At lunch I saw that Gemma was sitting with Nathan. Zack and Connor were still in the queue. I had to know what was going on. I'm not normally a nosey person as everyone knows, but I needed to know if Maddy was still in with a chance.

'He never asked her out you know.' Zack shook his head sadly. 'He never said a word to make her think they were going out.'

'You know we turned up just before the Coffee Bean closed?' Connor added.

'Did you?' I was surprised. 'But why?'

'He sounded desperate, so we did what good mates do and I got my mum to drive us in on a mercy mission.' Zack was ladling macaroni on his plate. Since an unfortunate incident involving Chris Jones's shirt and a plate of macaroni, I never touch the stuff.

Connor took up the story. 'Yeah, we turned up and said we're going to the cinema, and asked if he wanted to come. Which is what we'd decided would be the best thing to get him out of there. So Nathan looked at his watch, looked at Gemma and said, "Well it is closing." And she gave him this sharp look and said – Connor put on a girlie voice – "I'm sorry, Nathan; I thought we were in the middle of something. I have prepared all these ideas . . . I mean I was up till late last night making an effort on this leaflet to go with your poster, but if you want to go with your mates, if that's what you really want to do, that's fine, I just thought you were serious about animal welfare that's all . . ."

Zack said that she then went all hurt and sniffy and said she had some more stuff on the project at home. She was hoping he could spare just a few minutes . . .

Nathan had tried to say no, but she had acted so disappointed and hurt that eventually he had caved, saying that it *was* only for ten minutes. Gemma had dragged him out of the Coffee Bean and they heard nothing until Zack got a text two hours later saying Nathan had only just made it out of her house alive. When he heard she was telling everyone they were going out together, he was completely freaked out.

'Wow! What's he going to do now?' I queried.

'Gently but firmly put her straight, when he gets the right moment. Which has to be before the school trip and not in front of the whole class, which might be now so we're not going to sit with him. Don't want to hinder the process.'

So Zack and Connor came to sit on our table, but it wasn't a success because they were rude about Mr T's new rainbow tie-dye T-shirt and offended Rani and Chloe. I dread to think what they're going to say when they see us in ours. I feel my debt is repaid and I am off the hook now. And then I reminded them that Mr Trent had said 'a rainbow was a slide for tiny raindrops' and they said I had no soul.

But I do have soul. I have been thinking very seriously about things and in spite of my reservations about Mr T I have decided that, in between the mushy stuff, he does talk some sense. I am going to make changes in my house. I will be a Green Goddess after all. I am going to write a list.

★ 👓 CHLOE'S TIP: •
Don't give up on tights with small ladders or holes in them. Tie the ankles of these pairs so that you can quickly see that they are 'trousers only'. Saves time going through your drawer looking for a good pair as well.

Putting hand lotion on before handling tights helps stop snags.

Chapter 12

Tuesday 7.30 a.m.

First morning of new rules.

These are:

1. *Put the kitchen timer outside the shower and make people turn it to five minutes. It's a nice loud ring so you can hear it even when you are in the shower.*
2. *Put a brick in the cistern. (Which I have discovered is that thing behind the loo that's full of water.) You use less water with each flush that way.*
3. *Put notices in the bathrooms about turning the taps off when you're brushing your teeth.*
4. *Don't leave computers, CD players or televisions on standby, but switch them right off.*
5. *Be very strict about recycling paper, plastics, metal and glass in the right boxes.*
6. *Dad must not use his car and must go to the station on his bike (which he never uses – and it cost a fortune . . . he could have sold that for a couple of LA Alpha tickets easily).*

8.05 a.m.

Have had my chat with Mum about these, and frankly, I am disappointed. I felt her attitude wasn't quite up to the mark. She wasn't the slightest bit grateful that I noticed she hadn't heard her timer go off. Luckily for her I was there. She's been in a bad mood since she got out of the shower. I had to bang, bang on the bath-room door till she got out. I suggested she took the timer in with her in future, but she said she didn't want to, it might be danger-ous. She might get electrocuted. I pointed out it has a clockwork mechanism and then she said it might get rusty. Happily, Ned seems to have stopped washing at all lately (Rani says this hap-pened to her brother Norm at about the same age), so he saves loads of water just by himself. He seems to have abandoned the weird filming completely now and is back to skateboarding. He's also been asked to go for a proper audition by the casting agent for this school programme (are they mad?). This one is in London. Mum and Dad are taking him and I could have gone shopping with Mum in Oxford Street, but *no*, I will be in Deepest Devon up to my neck in mud and sea and dangling from cliffs and things.

Chloe and Rani have decided to go veggie. You would think their mums would welcome the opportunity to widen their cook-ing skills, but Rani says hers has been a bit disappointing on that front. I know what she means. Mine has found my insistence on only organic food, cooked from scratch, strangely challenging. You'd think she'd be glad to put in the extra effort for her own child. The only thing that has cheered her up is seeing Dad stand-ing in the kitchen in brand-new cycling helmet and trouser clips. Now *that* is an energy saving measure she's been *very* keen on. We have all just seen him off with a rousing cheer. As he wobbled off down the road Mum did say anxiously, 'I do hope we see him again.' That's typical: worry about my dad, but begrudge me my marinated tofu.

9.35 p.m.

In my bedroom surrounded by bags, ready to pack.

Have got all my clothes sorted for school trip. I had packed a whole lot more, including essential items like eyelash curlers and some outfits for the evenings, but Rani and Chloe had been very firm with me on this and made me abandon them. There is still the tie-dye T-shirt and neckscarf. Chloe's brother, Jim, fell in love with hers and she felt she had to let him have them. This meant Rani pleading and begging for me to take mine as she doesn't want to be the only one. I am truly the best friend in the world.

Tomorrow is the last day before we go to Devon. Last day of seeing Jack. Thank goodness it's not too long. Perhaps if Nathan has finished with Gemma already something might happen with Maddy while we are away? Wouldn't that be great?

 MADDY'S TIP: •
Although not everyone might be into tie-dyeing, you can revive old T-shirts by painting designs on them with fabric dyes. Customise them with the name of your favourite band, names, or just paint a picture. You can sew on buttons, sequins and ribbon as well.

Chapter 13

Wednesday 9.30 p.m.

I have said goodbye to Jack for four days. I wish he were coming too. I can't think of anything more romantic than walking along a beach with the waves crashing down, the wind in our hair . . .

I got very brave when we were walking through town to the bus stop.

'Will you miss me?' (I did say it in a casual ha ha ha sort of way.)

He did that Jack grin thing he does, swung my hand up and down, paused for a second, then said, 'Nope'.

It's very difficult not to laugh when he does this, but I wasn't going to let him get away with it this time.

'You so will. How could you *not*? It's four days and I *shall* be with the cream of Year Nine manhood.'

He was smiling broadly now. 'Ah well, when you put it like that . . .'

I raised my eyebrows at him.

He raised his back, then sighed. 'Of *course* I'm going to be pining away. In fact, I should think I'll be quite dead by the time you get back.'

And I thumped his shoulder. 'You'll be dead now if you don't shape up.' I laughed.

But suddenly he wrapped his arms around me and I saw that his face had clouded. 'It's only four days, Carrie.'

His voice made me nervous. 'What do you mean?' I asked.

'It's four days, that's not so long . . . I would hope we would last four days apart.'

That alarmed me. 'Of course we can, I was just . . . well, I'm sorry I asked now.' I went tomato-coloured. What the hell did he mean? Did he think I was too clingy? Did he think I was ridiculous to suggest he might miss me? I suddenly felt foolish. I pulled away. 'Do you know, I think I can get to the bus stop on my own, thank you. *And* manage four days apart. I'll see you when I get back from Devon then.' I stalked off down the road feeling crap and a little stupid. Then I heard him running up behind me calling my name.

'Look, I'm sorry, that didn't come out right; it's just that I've got something I need to tell you.'

My heart sank. Somehow those words tend not to come before good news.

'It's about the summer holidays.'

'What about them?

'My mum has arranged for me to go to Thailand and Malaysia for a holiday with her.'

'But that's great, isn't it?'

'For four weeks.'

'Four weeks!' I wailed. 'But that's practically the whole of the holidays.'

'I know, it's crap, but I can't not go. I don't really see her that much . . .'

'No, you've got to go. You'll have a great time.'

He put his arms around me. 'It'll go really fast, Carrie, you'll see.' He looked down at me. 'You OK?'

I took a deep breath. 'Yes, of course.'

We kissed again and then my bus came and he shouted out after me, 'Hey! You didn't say. Are you going to miss *me*?'

I turned around and managed to shout one word before the doors hissed shut: 'Nope!' I watched him laughing in the street as the bus drew away. I absolutely totally love Jack Harper. I do wonder what he really feels about me.

Other less important things that happened in the day: Mr Trent gave us a talk on some of the Devon activities, as if we didn't know what they were for goodness' sake.

My guide to Devon activities.

1. *'Kayaking'. Paddling a canoe up a river – how hard can that be?*
2. *'Coastal traverse – night-time'. Fancy way of saying walking along the beach in the dark and sitting round a fire. (See what I mean? Not tricky.)*
3. *'Abseiling'. Yes, probably the most difficult and I'm not crazy about heights, but I'm sure they'll just dangle you down in your harness if you don't want to do that leaning outwards thing, which I'm not sure I like the look of.*
4. *'Hiking'. They're having a laugh, aren't they? Everybody knows that's just a fancy word for walking. Don't know why they bother to mention it. I think we can all put one foot in front of another, can't we?*

Most depressing thing I discovered today (apart from Jack going away of course) was that Nathan was still going out with Gemma.

'He tried, Carrie.' Zack filled Chloe and me in on the details on the way to maths. 'But as soon as he said "Er, um, there's something we need to talk about, Gemma" she plunged straight in so he couldn't get another word out. "I'm *so* glad we're together, Nathan, it means so, so much to me. Especially as I've got my piano exam tonight and I'm so *nervous* about it and my family put so much *pressure* on me all the time about my music. I was so uptight about it I thought I was going to have to pull out, but now I'm with you, I just know that it's going to give me the confidence to pass."' Zack took a breath before continuing. 'And then she said, "If anything *bad* happens to me before the exam I know I would just fall to pieces and fail, but *nothing* bad is going to happen is it, Nathan? Not now we're going out?"'

'Wow, that's a bit heavy, isn't it?' I gasped.

'Sure is,' Zack said nodding. 'But it certainly worked. Nathan said he just couldn't do it. He's going to have to do it tomorrow after she's taken the exam. He really wants this misunderstanding sorted out before we go away.'

'Well he'll have to be quick about it. The coach leaves at half past nine,' Chloe observed.

Mmmm. I will never get Maddy her starter boyfriend at this rate.

Must check my packing. Again. Have left a long list of more green instructions for Mum for when I am away. Half an hour after I gave it to her I was horrified to see it in a pile of papers ready for the recycling bin. Luckily I rescued it and have pinned it up in the kitchen. I am very concerned that Mum, Dad and Ned may become rather slack when I'm not here to keep an eye on them. I feel they need a pep talk before I go tomorrow.

Tomorrow. What with one thing and another it's going to be an eventful day.

CARRIE'S TIP: • • • • • • • • • • • • • • • • • • •

Get your feet ready for beach exposure with all this natural treatment.

    4 teaspoons of sugar

    2 tablespoons of honey

    Mix together, and rub all over your feet (gives your hands a treatment at the same time). It's sticky so do this in a bath or on a towel and not your duvet. Rinse off and moisturise.

Chapter 14

We go today!

I am sitting on my bags in my room. Mum is taking me in to school.

Unpleasant start to the morning. It began with Dad, standing over me in his cycling helmet and trouser clips, waving a brick at me. And the brick was dripping all over my breakfast.

It is not my fault that when Mr Trent said put a brick (or something like it) in the toilet cistern, nobody told me it had to be a *special* brick. Dad replied it doesn't have to be a *special* brick, it just has to be a *clean* brick and not one I found behind the shed. Dad says it is not nice to go to the downstairs loo and see mud and grass clippings floating around in it. I got a bit desperate and said Mr Trent wouldn't mind. He is in touch with nature and finds the earth beautiful in all its manifestations. Everything doesn't have to be sanitised and sterile, you know. (Was that really me talking?) And Dad said that, *actually*, and call him old fashioned, he did feel that toilets should be on the clean side. And then he stomped off to the garage to get his bike.

Mum made me clean up the grass clippings, etc. Most of it did just flush away, thank goodness. Ned came to jeer. Ha ha. I complained to Mum. But Ned can do no wrong in Mum and Dad's eyes at the moment. He is Mr 'I'm going to London for an audition'. I am nothing but a slave. Thank goodness I am going away for a few days where I might be appreciated and it isn't all about being talented and being on camera. One thing you can say about Mr Trent I suppose, is that he isn't obsessed with outward appearances, but instead truly believes that beauty comes from within.

10.00 a.m.

On the coach.

Hugged Mum goodbye in the car park, amid the throngs of others doing the same. Noticed everyone looking very *au naturelle*. Even Jet was in jeans, flat sandals (!) and T-shirt. A sight never before seen at Boughton High. The biggest shock, however, was the teachers. Miss Gwatkins had dyed her hair! Miss Gwatkins has had peroxide blond hair for as long as anyone knew. Today it was a rather dark brown with an orange-y undertone. 'Just thought I'd like to go back to my natural colour,' she told Sarah Li's mum. But really we could tell she wanted Mr Trent to notice. He didn't seem to. Due to his spiritual non-shallow character I guess. Miss Gwatkins looked disappointed. I think she would like him to be a bit shallow sometimes. The second shock was Mrs McGuy. Gone was the tweed skirt, which was a surprise because I thought it was welded to her bod. Instead, the horror! She had on tweed knickerbockers, sturdy woollen socks and one-thousand-year-old leather walking boots. Aargh! Of course she couldn't have cared less what anyone thought about it. Must be bliss not to suffer from self-doubt. I felt a fleeting sense of envy.

Huge drama just before we got on. Nathan was trying to get to talk to Gemma and she seemed to sense something was up because she wouldn't let him get a word in edgeways. I mean she literally wouldn't let him open his mouth, she kept interrupting. And when he kept trying she said, 'Nathan! What is it with you this morning, wanting to yackety-yak and being all strange. I don't want to talk now, we're just off for four days in the country-side, I hope you're not going to spoil it.' She gave him a shove, told him to 'Get on the bus' and he reluctantly stepped on to the coach and she hopped on after him. He was still trying to say something in his desperation not to let the moment go and, I don't know exactly what happened, but one minute she was on the coach steps and the next minute she sort of stopped and fell backwards. He tried to catch her, but she landed on the pavement, holding her ankle and howling.

Nathan clambered down horrified to ask if she was all right. 'No, I'm not all right,' she wailed. 'Why did you lunge backwards like that?'

Nathan looked horrified. 'I didn't, I mean – you sort of crashed into the back of me . . .'

Mr Trent came to see what was going on. He helped Gemma to her feet, but she shrieked in agony.

Mr Trent looked anxious. 'Gemma, if you can't walk, you can't come on this trip.'

Gemma took a deep breath. 'I think I can just about move, a bit. I've been looking forward to this trip for so long, please let me go.'

And then they had to phone her parents and they had to speak to Mrs McGuy and Gemma was adamant that she wanted to come and she didn't care if she wouldn't be able to do all the activities and Sarah Li's mum is a doctor and said her ankle wasn't broken so in the end she came. Nathan helped her hobble painfully aboard. She patted the seat next to her and he sat down. He is consumed with guilt. He is doomed.

Feel as if I have been on this bus for about a million years.

I am so bored. Is everyone else as bored as I am?

Rani has just pointed out to me that they are not. Jet, Melanie and a few others have been kneeling up on the back seat holding up pieces of paper with *She fancies you* written on it in the window, then pointing at whoever was next to them and collapsing in hysterics. Then Melanie made one, which said *Honk if you think I'm sexy* and cars began hooting (out of kindness one must suppose) and then Mrs McGuy pounded up the aisle in those boots and that was the end of *that* little diversion.

Zahir bet Doug Brennan he couldn't drink a whole huge bottle of Coke in one go. Doug won, but we all had the fascinating sight of watching it all come back up again on the verge of the motorway five minutes later. Mr Trent said we weren't stopping the bus again for *anyone else.*

Ten minutes later we pulled into a service station so that Mrs McGuy could ceremoniously crush Sasha Dooley's fag packet into powder in her massive gnarled hands and drop it into a bin. Sasha was getting her iPod out of her bag and it fell out. Mrs McG truly does have eyes in the back of her head.

Anyone who thinks that makes for a fascinating trip makes one person more than Rani. I think I shall eat my last quarter of sandwich that I have been saving for desperate times.

GOD, RANI! BACK OFF! YOU ARE LIKE A VULTURE!

Calm has resumed.

Maddy poked a cheese straw between our seats to distract her. It will only buy us another ten minutes or so, but it will be enough time for me to finish my cheese and pickle on wholemeal in safety.

Maddy is very kind. Which makes me wonder what on earth is going on and why some people are sitting together when they shouldn't be. I will have to write more when I have some *privacy*.

Yes, Rani, eat your cheese straw and stop being nosey.

7.10 p.m.

I am sitting on a bench in the grounds, appreciating the evening sunlight. We have got a break until supper.

Baxted Hall is a beautiful place and it was worth the coach journey and even hearing Jackie and Sarah singing 'The Wheels on the Bus go Round and Round' and thinking it was cute. The main house is huge and white and old (Edwardian, I think Miss Gwatkins said). There is a long sweep of lawn down to the road and then you can see the cliffs and the deep blue of the sea beyond.

When we arrived the day went like this:

4.00 p.m.
Arrived.

Everyone fell out of the coach and we were greeted by George. He is our leader.

George gave us all a talk about everything we are going to be doing. George has been in the army and is quite scary but you certainly feel he knows his stuff. He's about forty to forty-five (I don't know, after twenty-five it gets so hard to tell), medium height, barrel-chested, bald and he looked like he could pick up Mrs McG and run three times around the grounds with her. He looked that freakishly strong. His sidekick is Kirstie, who is Australian with thick blond hair, thick thighs you could crush cricket balls with and just a hint of a charming moustache. And then there is Sam and Eddie, two South Africans who I have to say, though cute, look pretty tough as well.

I could see that anyone (e.g. Doug Brennan) who might have been thinking that this was all going to be a bit of a doss, was having a rapid rethink. Most of the other staff were Australian or South African and couldn't have been more welcoming or tanned – or healthy.

Apart from Chantelle. Who is the receptionist. How Chantelle got the job was a total mystery to us until it was revealed that she was George's daughter and was just covering for the girl who normally worked reception who had gone back to Australia for a funeral. Chantelle was into extensions, hair, nails and eyelashes, and I suspect boobs as well. They were on the unmissable side. Her blouse, which had obviously bravely struggled to reach the summit of her enormous bazookas had apparently become exhausted with the effort and had fallen back down the mountainside defeated, exposing a lot more than we really wanted to see. We all had to stand behind Mr Trent as he did our final check in and took in our mobile phones. I don't know why we can't have them. It's not prison or anything. And how will I keep in contact with Jack? Doug Brennan used his last seconds with his mobile to film Chantelle's frontage. I felt a flicker of negativity flit Mr T's positive life force as he firmly wrenched it from him. Mr T apologised profusely, but she thought it was funny. I'm surprised he wasn't blown across the room with the wind her eyelash-fluttering must have generated. To no avail. I could see Miss

Gwatkins patting her brown locks and looking pleased. Chantelle clearly didn't know that she was as far away from a Rainbow Ridge girl as it was possible to be.

4.35 p.m.
Cabin allocation. Ours is the furthest away from Mrs McGuy, which is good news. Mr Trent and Mr Goodge and the other male staff are with the boys in the cabins on the other side of the house.

5.30 p.m.
Huzzah! We were allowed to go swimming in the big outdoor pool. I was mightily relieved to be in my new pink cossie (so glad I eventually persuaded Mum) as not *one* other single person was wearing their Boughton costume (I knew Mum was lying when she said they would be – always trust your instincts). So there we all were, 9M, in our swimming kit. It is very embarrassing not wearing a lot in front of everyone in your class. Unless you are Jet, who paraded up and down in her gold lamé bikini, until at *last* Doug Brennan pushed her in and she could go all shrieky. It was bliss to get into the water. After a long, hot journey the feeling of coolness and to be able to kick out and stretch cramped limbs was wonderful. Everyone soon forgot about being so self-conscious, though obviously I held a towel over my behind whenever I actually walked anywhere.

Later, sitting on the grass, wrapped in that towel, I observed Gemma chattering cheerfully away to Nathan on the other side of the pool. Her ankle was propped up on a cushion. They were sitting with Zack and Connor. All the boys looked a tad gloomy.

'Do you think he's ever going to be able to finish it now that she's told everyone who would listen that his push on the steps has ruined her trip?'

Chloe nudged me. 'Well, here's your chance to find out. Zack and Connor are coming our way. But I want you to know that I am still suspecting your motives . . .'

'Hi, Zack.'

'Hi, Carrie,' Zack said gloomily. ''Spect you've noticed our merry band.'

'Can't not notice it.'

'I blame him for not saying it sooner. I talked him through it. He was supposed to say, "Gemma, there's been a bit of a mis-understanding here, we've never been going out together, it's all been in your head, goodbye and leave me alone".'

I was with Zack on all of that.

'Now he thinks he caused her sprained ankle and she's really working the guilt trip. He says she keeps sighing that she's been looking forward to it for so long and the only thing that makes it bearable is the fact that they are together.'

'So is he going to wait till after the trip?!' I was horrified. All my plans ruined. 'First the piano exam, now this. How did she do by the way? Did his love help her pass?'

'Apparently it was cancelled at the last minute.'

'No!'

'Yes, indeed. How about that for bad luck?' Zack shook his head, and he and Connor went off to swim.

Chloe arrived back from her dip. She was looking anxious.

'Er . . . listen everyone, I just want to ask you if the story that Doug Brennan is spreading around about the escaped madman is true, or whether he's just winding me up?'

'He'll be winding you up, Chloe, ignore him,' Rani said, then went on with what she had been talking about. Kirstie had told her there was a badger set in the woods. Rani wanted to go out one night and watch for them. Doug, drying his hair with his towel had wandered over to us and was listening.

'What! Are you mad, Rani! Do you want the *Breather* to get you?'

Rani snorted. 'What are you on about? What the hell is the Breather?'

'Haven't you been listening to the news? He's escaped from the prison on the moor. It's for the looniest of the loony. He's been locked in solitary confinement in that place, chained at all times, for twenty years. He's one of the most dangerous prisoners they have ever had.'

'Yeah right.' Rani laughed. 'And why is he called the Breather?'

'Because they say he has strange, heavy, rasping breath. And they say if he is close enough for you to hear it, IT IS TOO LATE.'

It was a bit of a creepy story; even though we were nearly one hundred per cent sure it was rubbish. It did give us the shivers, though. Especially Chloe, who is very sensitive. We are going for supper now. Good. I am starving, starving, starving.

10.45 p.m.

In our cabin.

I can see the whole room from my top bunk if I shine my torch around. Outside, the clouds have covered the moon and it is that spooky blackness of the countryside.

Rani is below me. She has stuck her foot out and is twirling her ankle around ve-ry slow-ly. She imagines this might make me laugh but I WILL NOT LAUGH. I will not make any noise at all. My hopes that not being in the closest cabin to Mrs McGuy might be an advantage have proved over-optimistic. She has been in twice already and I don't want to risk another visit. Especially as she might be in her jimmy-jams by now and honestly the sight would be more than flesh and blood could stand. In the top bunk on one side of me, Tess is lying with her legs straight up in the air because she doesn't want her fake tan to streak. Below her, Cara is already dropping off to sleep. Chloe and Maddy are in the bunk on the other side of me. Chloe is on the top one. When I shine my torch on Chloe's face I can see her lying awake, staring at the ceiling.

She has just asked me to stop shining my torch in her face, as it is quite annoying. I said I was only being kind, checking if she had managed to get to sleep. She said that she would never manage to get to sleep if every time she was about to drop off a megawatt beam of light dazzled her. This is a vast exaggeration as my torch is nowhere near that powerful, but I appreciate that Chloe is feeling creeped out and nervous about Doug's stupid story and it might be hard for her to relax.

Well maybe not – I've just shone my torch on her again and she's fast asleep. And I must stop now. I have a very active day tomorrow. My tie-dye T-shirt and neckscarf lie a-waiting for me. Luckily it's a hike in the morning to see the local terrain. So a bit of a rest day really.

Tip for travelling. Before you go, decant your shampoo, body lotion, conditioner, etc. into small plastic bottles. They'll be lighter and won't break. Two other good ideas are to save up all the trial-size sachets they give away free in magazines and to ask for the free samples they keep behind the beauty counters in department stores. Be practical *and* gorgeous!

Chapter 15

Friday 8.00 a.m.

Slept badly. Woke up in the night with distinct feeling that someone was watching us from the cabin window. Something had disturbed me. Flashed my torch around the room but everyone else was sleeping soundly. I heard Cara turn over. Knew I would not be doing anything brave like getting up, or anything foolish that involved moving at all, so decided to go back to sleep. This morning the sound of rain drumming on the roof and rattling the windowpane soothed my fears. That must have been what woke me. I am glad I didn't disturb the others now. I see how silly I had been. And anyway, I didn't want to fuel Chloe's anxieties again as this morning she was very perky and seemed to have forgotten Doug's story.

Rain really is quite heavy. It is obvious that the stroll, oops, sorry – *hike* – will be cancelled. We are off to breakfast (huzzah! I am starving again – that's the sea air for you). Then we will have our morning meeting. George will no doubt let us know what the alternative arrangements are. I am thinking a visit to the tuck shop and a bit of light table tennis might be just the job.

9.45 a.m.

I am in shock. The hike is still on. In *this* weather!

People are looking enviously at Gemma's ankle. She will be in the office with Chantelle while we are away. Reading mags and drinking tea in the cosy warmth.

We thought about a rebellion after George had broken the bad news, but then Mr Trent appeared looking rugged in waterproofs and his jeans tucked into huge wellies.

'It's very wet out there.' He smiled shaking the rain from his hair. 'But it's not so windy now and I think it's going to ease off. So what do you say? Who wants to experience the elements? It's so exhilarating.'

So of course all the girls went, 'Oooh yes, Mr Trent.' And the boys didn't want to be seen as wimps so that was that. The hike is on. Rani insisted I wear my huge cotton neckscarf as well as my tie-dye T-shirt. Zack grinned broadly when he saw us. 'Aah, you're like twin rainbows brightening up our dull day.'

I glared at Rani when we went back to the cabin, but she can be very aggressive for a small person and very pleading so here I am, the rainbow fairy. I am putting off going outside. I do not want to be seen standing next to her again as we look like Tweedledum and Tweedledee – quite ridiculous, in spite of Maddy and Chloe lying and saying we look fine, but I know Chloe's trying-not-to-laugh face too well. Yes, she can laugh now, safe in the knowledge her scarf is far away being loved and appreciated by her brother.

Rani says the most important thing is that Mr Trent notices them.

You see this is what you get for being kind. Dr Jennings, please take note. I tried to be a good friend and where is my reward? Nowhere.

2.45 p.m.

We are back. No one could imagine the experience I have just had. People sniggering at Rani and me turned out to be the least of my worries. I ache in places I didn't know I *had*. I have absorbed more water than is humanly possible. I have been marched up precipices and over rocks, I have been tramped across bogs and fallen down a rabbit-hole. I have *not* been allowed to do the most logical thing, which was to stop walking, lie down in the grass and go to sleep. In spite of my pleading. And all this whilst carrying my backpack, water bottle and the equivalent of one large, wet sock around my neck. And it got wetter and wetter and water started to trickle down my back. I unwound it, caught Rani up, who was trudging gamely ahead in order to impress you-know-who, and wrung it out on her head. That was when she pushed me into the hole.

I am now lying on my bunk. I have had a shower. I have tried to wash off the pink and purple stain around my neck, but a faint ring still lingers. Rani also looks like someone tried to strangle her. So much for colour-fast dye. I will not be moving for the foreseeable future. Mr Trent, Mrs McGuy and George led us through the gates of Baxted Hall like cheery Pied Pipers. Fit types like Sasha and Maddy still managed to look cheerful, whilst the rest of us limped home like the exhausted, whimpering, wet rats we were. When Mr T said, 'Wasn't that great, guys? Don't you feel in awe of the power of the natural world?' Chloe noticed even Miss Gwatkins's smile looked a bit forced.

Have to move now because there are buns, hot buttered toast and cakes laid out in the dining hall and though every step will be agony, my body is a temple and I must respect its wishes.

3.45 p.m.

Feel better after refuelling.

A pale watery sun has appeared behind the thinning grey

clouds. Kayak practice in the pool is back on the agenda. Our wet clothes are in the driers. Our T-shirts and scarves are on the radiators so as not to contaminate other garments. We are being allowed a little break before getting changed for kayaking, which seems to require a lot of kit and strapping in. And more water. The good news is that after plenty of toast and two slices of cake, and several mugs of hot, sweet tea, I think my body can stand it.

Cara said something at tea that bothered me. Rani had done a big stretch and said, 'I'm going to sleep like a log tonight. The sea air is like a sleeping pill, isn't it?'

'I know,' Cara replied. 'I need it after last night. It must have been the rain on the roof, but I just had this feeling that someone was *watching* me.'

I must have gone red or sat up or something because quick as a flash Rani said, 'What's up, Carrie? Was it *you* watching her? You perv.'

'Duh, *no*, you twit! What the hell would I be doing watching Cara in the middle of the night?'

'So what's up then? Why did you look all spooked when Cara said that?'

'I didn't!'

Rani gave me patient look. 'Carrie, we all know you can't act so you might as well tell us. Did you think someone was watching you too? Did you think it might be . . .' – she inhaled deeply and rasped – '*the Breather*?'

'No.'

'Oh my God you did!' gasped Chloe. 'You thought he was watching you too! Someone was outside our cabin. Did you hear . . . did you hear . . .'

'No, we didn't hear any *breathing*.' Cara laughed. 'Don't get into a panic, Chloe, it was the combination of the rain and being in a strange place. Look, we obviously both knew that, we went straight back to sleep and dah dah!' She gestured at herself. 'Are we fine? Yes! Perfectly fit and well. So let's not get freaky about this, OK, or I will get mad. *Understand*?'

Chloe nodded, but I knew she wasn't convinced. Rani doesn't get spooked about anything silly like creepy stories and she was kind enough not to tease Chloe about it. Instead she said, 'Maybe it was a teacher doing a late night check on all of us, we had had Mrs McG in twice – maybe she was doing a final look through the window to make sure we had really gone to sleep.' I wish I could be as confident. I know she must be right. Of course she is.

Must go kayaking now.

8.00 p.m.

Kayaking was fun, but Mr Trent has a new fan and it is seriously annoying all his old ones. Chantelle is *everywhere*. I mean not on the hike or anything (those heels!), but *everywhere* around the place. She has got her dad to let her come on the kayaking trip tomorrow. She's now asking *us* about him. She tracked us down to the laundry room when Rani, Chloe, Maddy and I were collecting our dry clothes.

'That's right, girls, you get your things, I've done that Mr Trent's already. He's lovely, isn't he?'

Rani looked at me and raised her eyebrows.

'Can't wait for the rowing or whatever tomorrow. I'm telling you it'll be better than being stuck in the office with that little madam. Had me running around her like I was her slave or something. I tell you, I feel sorry for that boyfriend of hers she never stopped going on about, he's that good to her. Lovely personality, like your Mr Trent . . . Bet you've all got a crush on him. I know I would have. When I was your age.'

Maddy gave her a level look. 'He's our *teacher*,' she said coolly.

'What?! Yeah, course he is. Course he is. Do you know if he's got a girlfriend? That Miss Gwatkins, she watches him like a hawk. Oh my God! He's not going out with her, is he?'

'GIRLS!' It was Mrs McGuy standing at the door, giving Chantelle a megawatt glare. 'Could you please hurry up and get to your cabins immediately while I have a quick word with —'

But Chantelle had ducked out of the door with a 'Dear oh dear, is that the time? I'll be in right old trouble if I don't get back to my desk right this very minute.' Leaving Mrs McG breathing fire out of her nostrils.

'God,' Rani sighed when we got back to our cabin. 'She is the dimmest person I've ever met.'

'You don't know that for sure,' Maddy said kindly.

'I do,' Rani snorted. 'When I asked her if Baxted Hall did recycling she said she didn't think so, but they did do mountain biking one year.'

I felt a bit uncomfortable. 'Well, I'm not sure if we gave all that much thought to that sort of thing before this term.'

'Yes, but she's much older than us. She must be at least twenty-five. She's got no excuse and all that make-up and heaving bosom. Mr Trent must shudder when he sees her coming.'

'Well, I know Miss Gwatkins does.' I smiled. 'Mind you, he doesn't seem that interested in Miss Gwatkins either.'

'Of course not,' Rani sighed. 'Neither of them are the right person for him. Anyone can see *that*.'

It made me think about Jack and hope that he thought I was the right person for *him*. I do hope so, it's so hard to tell these things. I wonder what he's doing now?

We are getting ready to go and eat and then we are going to see a film in the recreational room. I could go to sleep now and skip the film, but I want to make sure I'm really, really tired tonight.

Rani has just lifted her chin from the T-shirt she was pulling over her head. 'River has much more important things on his mind than passing relationships. I think he is waiting for someone very, very special and he may not find that person for years and years . . .'

Chloe nodded. 'Very, very true, Rani.'

I despair. Where is Rani's pink pencil? She needs a prod.

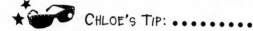 CHLOE'S TIP: ● ● ● ● ● ● ● ● ● ● ● ● ● ● ● ● ● ●

If you are not hiking in the rain you can give your circulation a boost another way by applying body lotion in circular movements from the ankle up. Very good for keeping skin looking toned and healthy.

Chapter 16

The film worked. (*Grease*. Made me think of Ned and wonder how his audition went.) I slept like I was in a coma. I think a hundred Breathers could have been having a party outside and I wouldn't have heard it. I was physically exhausted. And now a big bowl of cereal and eggs on toast is calling me. The sun is shining and we're all slapping on the Factor 40 because no one wants to be burned to a frazzle on the river.

During supper last night (shepherd's pie and green beans – veggie option available), we watched Nathan help Gemma limp to a seat and then go and get her something to eat. '*She's loving every minute of it!* She's driving me nuts with this invalid thing.' It was Jet scraping back the empty chair next to me. I was just getting used to seeing her without make-up and designer clothes. With some natural colour in her face from yesterday's exertions and just a simple white T-shirt and jeans, she looked a totally different girl. Melanie joined her.

'What are you talking about, Jet?' Rani exclaimed. 'I thought she was your best friend and passport to footballer heaven.'

Jet snorted. 'Yeah right! You'd think she might feel she owed us something for setting her up with Nathan. But now she's got her clutches on him it's like she doesn't want to know us! She's been turning her nose up whenever we try and just say hello. I wish I'd let *you* have him, Carrie.'

I gasped. 'It wasn't like *that*. *I'm* not interested in him . . .'

'Whatever.' Jet shrugged. 'But I wish I hadn't bothered all the same.'

'I think she thinks *we're* after him,' Melanie screeched and the two of them said in unison, 'as if!'

Jet looked over at Gemma yakking away to a subdued Nathan and scowled.

'Why don't you cut out the middleman, sorry, *girl*, and just ask Nathan if he could get his dad to get you a backstage pass, or whatever the football equivalent is?' a tired Chloe queried. (She had lain awake a lot of the night – although she admitted she heard nothing strange.)

Jet gave her a patronising sneer. 'Yeah and we hadn't thought of that ourselves.' She began to tick off on her fingers. 'One, you know he's not that mad about Melanie or me due to our total lack of interest in him, ever. We think that might spoil our chances of him doing us any favours. It's obvious now we're only being nice to get in with his dad. And two, as if Gemma will let us anywhere near him now anyway. And she doesn't care who his dad is or anything about footballers. A total waste.'

'I know,' Melanie chorused. 'Talk about lack of blimmin' gratitude. Who does she think she is?'

Jet's eyes narrowed. 'Well, she better watch out because if I ever get something on her, she'll regret she ever ditched us like we were nothing. *Really* regret it.'

And I actually felt a little bit sorry for Gemma. You don't start treating Jet as if she were dirt under your shoe and expect to get away with it.

8.00 p.m.

I am lying on my bunk all dressed up for tonight's disco. (Shorts and T-shirt.)

The physical strain of the day has taken its toll on me.

It began in the bright sunshine; we were all standing outside the boathouse putting our kayaking kit on. (And those helmets are sooo not flattering.)

'Oh. My. God.' Rani's eyes were popping out of her head.

The jaws of every girl in 9M hit the top of their life jackets.

George paused from checking that the boys' jackets were properly fitted and beamed. He called out, 'Hello, love, nice to see you taking an interest at last.'

Chantelle was tottering across the lawn towards us. Mr Trent brushed a dark lock of hair from his face and paused in pulling on his jacket over his head. An expression I could not quite read passed across his face. Then he continued to get ready.

'See,' whispered Rani, 'he thinks she's horrendous. What is she *thinking*?'

Miss Gwatkins's expression was interesting. Think chewing lemons. Chantelle *was* impossible to ignore. She was wearing a teeteringly high pair of cork wedges ('To be used as floats in case of emergency?' Chloe whispered), a T-shirt about three sizes too small and a pair of shorts of such teeny-weenyness that when she turned around to go back to the house with her dad to get some sensible shoes, there was a collective gasp from all the assembled group – one of horror from the girls and of admiration from most of the boys. That was a *lot* of cheek on show. Kirstie raised her fulsome eyebrows and began to hustle everyone on board the minibuses that were trundling our equipment and us further down the river. Of course there was huge competition to go with Mr Trent, but he was taking so long to get ready that Rani had to fake not being able to get her life jacket on properly to get us places on the bus with her idol. Jet just simply hid with Melanie behind a van until everyone else was safely dispatched. Rani and Jet's battle for beautiful spiritedness is still very much on.

George and Chantelle came back and he delivered his daughter to our bus before joining the one in front. This time Chantelle was in a sensible pair of trainers.

'Bloody hell,' she laughed as she climbed aboard, 'I can hardly walk. I haven't worn flat shoes since I was a toddler. Just as well you're here to look after me, isn't it?' She held on to the tanned forearm of the assisting Mr T for just a moment too long. 'Ooh. Do you work out?'

Mr T looked serious. 'I think it's important to keep fit. We only have one body and we must try to look after it.'

Chantelle turned and gave us a wink. '*I'll* say.'

'Disgusting!' Rani muttered, folding her arms and leaning back in her seat. She added that if Mrs McGuy were on the bus to witness such inappropriate behaviour she'd probably have Chantelle arrested for sexual harassment or something.

She then stared fixedly out of the window, sulking. She was not alone. Most of the girls on this bus had fought hard for their moment with Mr T. Including Miss Gwatkins. Now it was being hijacked. Chantelle, cheerily unaware of the waves of hatred coming her way, chattered merrily to Mr T in her high-pitched squeak.

I nudged the sulking Rani. 'Don't be cross, he's only listening to be polite. He can't very well ignore her, can he? She *is* the group leader's daughter.'

'I know,' she hissed. 'But it's just so embarrassing that someone as sensitive as him has to listen to that . . . that *nonsense*.'

'You know,' Chloe added, 'he thinks everyone is special in their own way. He's a very kind and sensitive man. Maybe her voice doesn't affect him in the same way it does us.'

'Like fingernails scraping down a blackboard you mean,' sniffed Rani.

Maddy sighed. 'Tell me again *why* he's so great.'

'I told you before, he has *soul*,' Rani replied.

'And he's deep, he doesn't go for appearances but cares about what you're like inside,' Chloe added.

'And he's dead fit,' Jet chipped in.

'And he's made us see that "artificial adornment is like painting the butterflies and the flowers in nature's garden",' Sarah quoted reverentially.

I put my fingers over my ears. 'Stop it, I'm begging you. I'm going to puke.'

'Are you ill, Carrie?' I looked up to see Mr Trent watching me with an alarmed look on his face. 'I've got some grated ginger and hot water in my flask; it's very good for nausea.'

'Er no. You're all right. I'm fine now.'

'Cool.' He smiled. 'Because we're like, here.'

Botheration. I will have to write about the kayak trip later. Rani has reached up from her bunk and is shaking my ankle. It's disco time (whoopee). More later.

10.45 p.m.

Back in bed at last. It's go, go, go all the time in this place. Which is just as well because it takes my mind off CREEPY THINGS that might stop me going to sleep. And talking of creepy things I have just had the horrendous and very stressful experience of seeing Miss Gwatkins go up against Chantelle on the dance floor at our little disco.

Now where was I? Right. The river. Was that only this morning? Seems like a century ago.

I wanted to spend my time on the water usefully. This meant finding a moment to talk to Maddy about the Nathan/Gemma situation and reassuring her that Nathan would surely come to his senses soon.

We launched the kayaks into the water and set off. Rani sped ahead to keep close to Mr T, along with Jet, Melanie, Miss Gwatkins and Chantelle. Chantelle was hopeless of course, having not had our swimming pool practice session. Much shrieking and clinging to the side of Mr T's canoe. I could see Miss G had to use all her powers of self-restraint not to clobber her over the head with her paddle. In the end the wonderful Kirstie edged smoothly alongside and took over instructing her. This allowed Mr T to drift into one of his speeches about the riches of the river and, like, the amazing cleanliness of the water. Which was true. It flowed under us, crystal clear. You could see the speckled trout swimming underneath you in between the reeds swaying with the current. A gaggle of girls sighed after him like water nymphs following in the wake of some lesser river god.

I let myself drift behind for a few minutes asking Maddy to help me with my paddle technique.

I decided on the direct approach. 'What do you think of Nathan, Maddy?' I opened, staring intently at the bank as if I'd just seen a kingfisher or something else really interesting.

'Nathan? He's a really nice boy, real genuine. He's easily one of the nicest guys in the class.'

This perked me up no end. She *still* liked him, in spite of the Gemma thing.

'He's not really interested in Gemma, you know. Really not. Anyone can tell.'

Maddy frowned. 'Do you know, I think you could be right. He never seems to look that happy, does he?'

'Miserable, Maddy. He's absolutely miserable. He so obviously wants to finish it but feels too guilty about the ankle thing. It's not like a real relationship anyway – is she the only one who hasn't noticed he hasn't kissed her once? I mean, that's just friends where I come from.'

Maddy went the same colour as her life jacket. 'There's nothing wrong with being just friends. If you like someone a lot that can be enough.'

My paddle flicked a spray of water into my face. 'I know that, but what if you wanted to be *more* than friends with someone, Maddy . . .'

She straightened her back and started paddling faster. 'Well, if that person is going out with someone else there's not much you can do about it, is there? It's pointless and stupid and a waste of time to think about,' she added stiffly, brushing her thick dark fringe out of her eye with the back of her hand.

Panting, I tried to keep up. 'But if that person finished with that other person, what then?'

Maddy dipped her paddle vertically in the water and slowed right down. This time she was looking right at me.

'What do you mean?'

'I mean if you like someone a lot, a lot, *a lot*, Maddy, maybe you should tell someone, you know – get it off your chest.'

'Do you *know* something, Carrie? Do you think that I like somebody? Somebody who is going out with someone else? Because I've certainly never said anything that even hinted at that kind of situation to you . . .'

'I know, I know, but, um . . . yes.' I bit my lip nervously, you don't mess about with Maddy and I was on dangerous, *personal* ground here. 'But I think you *might*.'

Maddy flushed again, then clenched her jaw. 'Is it that obvious?' she growled. 'I must be less smart than I imagined.' She turned to me. 'I can't believe *you've* guessed!' (I have to admit there was a *tone* there I wasn't sure about.) 'God, does anyone else know?'

'We-ell,' I said modestly, 'no, no one else. No one but me has a tiny clue, so don't worry. It's just a sort of sixth sense I've got. I'm fantastically intuitive sometimes. I just *know things*.'

Maddy looked serious. 'Look, Carrie, I don't know *how* you've guessed as I certainly didn't tell anyone, but if you tell a single soul . . .'

'Cross my heart and hope to die,' I whispered, crossing my paddle in front of my chest, 'I swear.'

So you see I was right all along, like I always, always am. When I grow up I had thought of being a psychiatrist, but now I think I'll be an agony aunt on my days off. Or maybe they're the same thing anyway. I'll have to ask Dr Jennings. What this means is that my mission to get Maddy and Nathan together is now definitely on again.

In the bunk below, Rani is doing her creepy breathing again. I have told her to shut up. It's not funny.

She says it is. She says she's trying to lighten the mood.

It isn't working.

Maddy seemed to be so shocked that I guessed that she was keen on Nathan that she got all hot and bothered and in a few minutes was steaming ahead up the river. Rani and Chloe had fallen behind the others and we paddled together. Rani was spitting with rage. 'She's a Poison Pixie with a Paddle,' she hissed. 'Thank goodness Kirstie took her off his hands; he must have been desperate for someone to help him out. Why does she have to come with us anyway? She's not part of our school. Why can't she go on her own?'

'Ooh, you don't want to be anywhere on your own, Rani. Not now, not with the *Breather* closing in on us.' We had come alongside Doug and Eddie.

I gave Chloe a nervous glance. 'Shut up, Doug. There is no Breather; stop trying to spook us.'

Doug looked serious. 'I'm not kidding, Carrie. There really is. I wouldn't make up anything as freaky as that.'

'Oh yeah,' Rani sniffed. 'Prove it then. Prove to us that the Breather is not a figment of your tiny imagination.'

'I will.' Doug was moving along next to our kayak now.

'Oh right. And just how do you intend to do that?'

'I'll show you when we get back.' We had reached the bend in the river. It narrowed and the trees leaned dark and green over the banks. It was suddenly very quiet; the only sound the dip of the paddles.

'He stalks people for days, you know,' Doug murmured. 'Watching their movements. Creeping around the chalets in the dead of night I expect and probably tracking us now, peering out from behind the trees along the riverbank. Like a wolf watching a flock of sheep, waiting and waiting for one to get left behind. Alone and defenceless. And you have no idea he's there, lurking in the shadows, until you hear the first deep, hoarse breaths circling you . . . getting closer and closer until . . .'

A pheasant shot out of the trees in a panic of beating wings.

Chloe screamed.

'Until I smack you across the back of my head with this paddle,' Rani warned. 'Now stop this stuff before I get really annoyed.'

Doug sighed. 'The truth is the truth, girls. You can't fight Fact. Like I said. I'll show you when we get back.'

And then Kirstie, who had fallen way behind due to trying to teach Chantelle how to stop splashing and to actually move forwards, caught up with us and we all got barked at to get moving. If Chantelle asked, 'Are we nearly there yet?' once she asked it a trillion times. She was in a very bad mood now the object of her affections was far ahead of her. She had obviously not intended to spend her day under the firm supervision of Kirstie – the Australian Amazon and stranger to tweezers.

I was secretly with Chantelle. It was a very, very long way back and the basic design fault with kayaks is that if *you* stop moving, *they* stop moving. Someone needs to get back to the drawing board on that one.

I watched Miss Gwatkins's smile of triumph when we eventually got back and Chantelle staggered out of her kayak and silently (for once) staggered up into the Hall.

Mr Trent was in his element. He gathered us all together and showed us how he had collected reeds and feathers and tiny twigs along the way. He had woven the feathers and twigs into the reed and tied one around his neck. He had brought back a bundle of reeds and most of the girls were now gathering twigs and stuff off the ground and weaving their own. Miss Gwatkins appeared at the disco with her decorated reed tied around her head. Like a Native American. Not.

Maddy looked great in jeans and pretty cotton kaftan top. Pity she didn't get a chance to get anywhere near Nathan the whole evening. It must be so painful for her to see him with Gemma all the time. Gemma couldn't dance, obviously, but managed to look bravely martyred the whole evening, keeping Nathan at her side. Maddy is incredibly courageous about this difficult situation. It's quite romantic really.

Actually the disco was fun. Sam firmly resisted all Mr Goodge's attempts to take over the decks, so the music was good anyway. Mr Trent chatted to Kirstie and Miss Gwatkins, also known as Minnie-ha-ha. George wasn't at the disco and Chantelle, realising the coast was going to be clear, reappeared halfway through the evening in spiky boots, skintight jeans and a boob tube that was barely earning its name. Mr T, like King Solomon, made a wise decision not to dance and then the showing off started between Miss Gwatkins and Chantelle. And it was not a pretty sight for young people to witness and, frankly, neither of them was much of a dancer. But what they lacked in talent they certainly made up for with enthusiasm. It was cringeworthy enough to clear the dance floor of Year Nine in five minutes flat. Us teenagers are sensitive creatures you know.

It's no use; even my embarrassment at that memory has not made me forget the CREEPY THING. This evening Doug showed us his proof about the Breather. It is true! It was a photo-copied cutting from the local newspaper all about the escaped criminal, saying how dangerous he was and how he was 'not to be approached'.

I'm trying to be dead cool about it and not show I'm nervous. Chloe was quaking in her bed for ages, but I hope she's asleep now.

I'll just check.

'FOR THE THOUSANDTH TIME, WILL YOU STOP SHINING THAT BLOODY TORCH IN MY FACE AND GO TO SLEEP, CARRIE!'

That is the thanks I get for trying to be a caring friend.

 MADDY'S TIP: •

For a healthy 'I've been outdoors' glow, grind a handful of rose petals into a paste with a little milk, and, if you have dry skin, add a teaspoon of honey.

Apply to clean skin and leave for fifteen to twenty minutes. Wash the paste off with water (no soap) and admire your smooth, radiant, soft skin.

Chapter 17

Sunday 6.00 a.m.

Yes, it is early, but I have hardly slept. We have had A NIGHT OF TERROR.

At about 1.00 a.m. I was woken up by Rani shaking my shoulder. I sat bolt upright.

'What?! What?'

'Shhhh . . . be quiet. I don't want to wake Chloe. She'll panic. Get up and come into the bathroom with me. Where we won't disturb the others.'

She was shaking and pale.

'I'm panicking here, Rani. What the hell is going on?' We were in the bathroom now. Rani shut the door gently behind her.

'I went to the loo.'

'Right, well that's going to terrify anyone.'

'Shut up. I saw something out of the bathroom window . . . Something crossing the grass and disappearing into the woods.'

'Some*thing*?'

I could see that Rani was genuinely scared. I clutched her hand.

'It was a . . . a *person*,' she whispered.

'Like a human-being-type person?'

Rani gave me a look.

'Really and truly?' I went on. 'You're sure?'

'Yes, of course I'm sure,' she hissed. 'I wouldn't wake you up in the middle of the night for a joke . . .'

'Well, there was that sleepover when you dressed up as the killer nun . . .'

'Oh for goodness' sake, Carrie!'

'We've got to tell Mrs McGuy and Mr Trent.'

'I know. That's why I woke you up. I want you to come with me.'

Then someone tried the bathroom door handle. Rani's hand was still on it. She held on tightly and tried to resist the force pushing against her. But she couldn't and slowly it began to open. Rani looked like she was about to scream and my heart was jumping all over my chest.

Maddy's dark head appeared cautiously around the door.

'What's going on?'

Rani and I slumped against the wall in relief.

'Hellfire, Maddy, you nearly made me die of fright.'

'So . . . you didn't answer my question. What's going on?'

'Rani saw someone creeping into the woods.'

Maddy frowned. 'Seriously? Are you sure?'

'Yes, of course I'm sure! I'm not an idiot, you know.'

'Did you see what they looked like?'

'No! It was so dark, I could only just make out a figure in the moonlight and it was a long way away.'

Maddy's face relaxed. 'Are you sure it was a person, Rani? There are loads of deer around here. Perhaps it was a deer who had come out to graze, just going back into the woods.'

'Well, it was a deer walking on its hind legs then,' Rani snapped.

So we all three tiptoed out past the sleeping forms of Cara, Tess and Chloe. I got my torch. We crept out looking carefully in all directions, but nothing was moving. The dew on the grass was cold on our bare feet. I led the way, singing 'All Things Bright and Beautiful' quietly under my breath for protection. Not generally known as a protection song, but it was the only one I could think of. I began to wish Mrs McGuy's cabin was a bit nearer to ours after all and our walk quickly turned into a run and in no time we were hammering on the door of Mrs McGuy's teacher cabin.

'You'd have thought she would have been more sympathetic, wouldn't you?' Rani said when all the hoo-ha had died down.

'Absolutely. Especially towards young people seeing a teacher in their jimmy-jams and dressing gown. Did you notice it was a *tweed* dressing gown?'

'I bet her panties are made of tweed, you know,' Maddy added.

'OH MY GOD, MADDY! I know that you are an American person and all that, but never, never, use the word "*panties*" in the same sentence as "Mrs McGuy" ever, ever again. Promise?'

'What should I say? Knickers?'

'Knickers would have been better, but the best thing of all would be to say neither.'

'I feel silly now,' Rani groaned. 'I got you all up and Mrs McGuy and Mr Trent and Sam and Kirstie.'

'It wasn't your fault. You saw someone going into the woods. Of *course* we had to tell someone. We were terrified. And what if it *had* been the Breather and not Chantelle after all . . .' I gave her a hug.

'And how could anyone have guessed that a girl like that would be the sort of person who might be interested in going to watch badger cubs at night?' Maddy said, yawning.

'Well, she said Kirstie told her about them too, and when she started going on about how "ickle and furry" they were, you could sort of see it, I suppose.' Now I was yawning too.

'At least we can sleep peacefully,' I said cheerfully. 'Mystery solved.'

'Let's hope so,' Rani said darkly.

'Rani! It was her. Mr Trent searched those woods for ages and there was no one else around. You just assumed it was ... you-know-who, but it was dark, you couldn't see much. And she didn't hear a thing to worry her in the woods. She was ALONE.'

'Well, she shouldn't have been. Alone in those woods at night? Anything could have happened.' Rani paused. 'Mr Trent was super brave, wasn't he?'

Even I had to agree there. When we had banged on his door with Mrs McGuy he had luckily come to the door fully dressed; he'd been working on a new song about the river.

'The words were flowing like the water itself, I just, like, couldn't let that inspiration go to waste. It would have been like letting a beautiful flower disappear ...'

In spite of our warnings he'd shown no fear at all and plunged straight into the woods saying, 'The dark is our friend, we shouldn't fear it ...'

Then Chantelle had appeared out of the trees a few minutes later. He had found her watching the badger cubs. She was laughing her head off. She obviously thought that the whole thing was completely hilarious, but reassured us that the woods were perfectly safe and she hadn't encountered any strange men. 'More's the pity!' she cackled and toddled off back to the Hall. She may like fluffy badger cubs, but she certainly wasn't dressed for the woods at night. Mr Trent was our hero. I could tell even Mrs McGuy thought she had misjudged him. She did say our story about the Breather was utter nonsense and she'd be doing some investigating as she walked us back to our cabin. The others were all still sleeping soundly.

Maddy whispered from her bunk, 'She didn't mind being alone in the woods because this is her home. She must know them like the back of her hand. It's not like for us, all strange and different. She's lived here for years . . .'

'Not exactly nature's child though, is she?' Rani grumbled.

'Shhh!' Maddy ordered. 'Let's get some sleep while we still can, it's nearly light now anyway.'

And I did drop off, but woke up this early; must be all that adrenalin pumping round my body.

I am going to try and get an hour or so more sleep before we have to be up and ready for abseiling. That's another thing that's making me nervous.

I just need to do one more thing before I nod off.

I have just tipped my head over the edge of the bunk.

'Carrie, if you don't stop shining that bloody torch in people's faces I will not be responsible for my actions.'

'Just checking,' I tutted.

3.00 p.m.

Lying in the sunshine, on the grass next to the pool.

Chantelle had obviously woken up this morning with one thing in mind: to blab the whole story of last night's escapade to everyone she could. By the time the last spoonful of cereal was shovelled in, everyone knew. Mr Trent was the hero of the night, of course. I think it went to his head a bit because he got all athletic at the bottom of the abseiling tower (think very high structure, possibly with Rapunzel letting down her golden hair from the top) and started hanging out really far in his harness. He looked pretty cool and was obviously rather pleased with himself because he'd never done any of this sort of climbing before. 'Must just come naturally to some people,' he murmured. Rani and the others were practically fainting at his panther-like grace.

Abseiling is like this: after a while of lulling you into a false sense of security on the lower slopes they say, 'OK, everyone, we're moving now.' And up you go.

TO YOUR DOOM.

George double-checked everyone was 'clipped in' and then basically they pushed us poor defenceless children over the side into a bottomless abyss. Well, not physically pushed, more mentally harassed us until we broke down.

Everyone was waiting for Mr T to show us some fancy tricks as he was first to bound up the steps, but as he neared the top he slowed right down and got very busy encouraging other people to go past him, and then he went rather quiet.

Nathan shouted from his nearly upside-down position just below, 'Are you coming, sir? Are you coming? It's amazing! Come on, sir!'

So nice to see Nathan free at last. Gemma was sitting outside on the grass waiting like a cat waits for a mouse to come out of its hole.

Mr T held up one hand, the other holding on to the railing. 'Do you know, guys, it looks like the best time, but I think that

I'm really needed down at the bottom, you know, to, like, make sure everyone appreciates what an amazing thing they have achieved. To really let them feel some positive vibes . . . I'd love to join you, but I just think that that's the more important thing . . .'

'Oh sir!' Rani and Chloe wailed in unison. He raised his free hand higher. 'I know, I know, but you have to understand where I'm coming from on this; it's not about me here,' he sighed and nodded soulfully at us. 'It's about *you*.'

We are allowed to have a swim now and then tea. I am starving. It is hours since lunch. I need a scone with lots of butter and jam. I need two. And some hot toast. They are going to drive us further down the coast to the start of the coastal traverse. This means walking along the dunes, ending up on the beach near here. Nice flattish walking. By the time we reach the beach it will be dark and George, Sam and Kirstie are going to organise a barbecue around a big bonfire. The rest of the staff will be walking with us. The neckscarves are out again. Rani says it's our last night, and the dye won't run any more – all the colour that was going to come out came out on the hike – and maybe Mr Trent will notice this time. Everyone has to take a torch. Trouble is the batteries are low on mine due to much late night diary writing and checking on Chloe. I have spares. I must change them.

Chloe says I don't need to check on her any more, thank you, as the mystery of the night wanderer has been solved.

Actually I don't remember Chantelle saying that she had been down to the woods *before* last night. But I'm not going to think about that now.

 CARRIE'S TIP: •••••••••••••••••••••••••

If you've been out of doors a lot or you are not drinking
enough water, your lips can get dry and chapped. To help get
them smooth again, put on Vaseline and brush gently with a
clean, *soft* toothbrush (you don't want to do any damage to
your poor lips – you're trying to help them). Blot off excess
Vaseline with a tissue.

Chapter 18

Sunday 10.35 p.m.

Safely back in the cabin.

I will need therapy for about a thousand years to get over the coastal walk with barbecue. Dr Jennings won't be able to write it all down fast enough. I don't think I will get over it.

Ever.

I'm surprised the others can sleep; my heart is still beating so loudly.

It all started with the Gemma/Nathan thing. With all the whining about her ankle we'd had to put up with over the past few days it seemed obvious to everyone that she wouldn't be able to come on the walk. She would have to go and be rude and patronising to Chantelle in the office again. Even though she tried very hard to make Nathan feel guilty again and stay with her, Mrs McGuy stepped in and said that she was not having a perfectly fit and well boy missing out on the walk. Sometimes I think Mrs McG has flashes of wisdom. Sometimes. I knew that meant Nathan out of Gemma's sight for a few hours. I worked out a plan to wheedle it for Maddy to walk with him, so they could get to know each other better, etc., etc. I naturally had to abandon any ideas of them snogging long ago. But I felt it would lay foundations for THE FUTURE.

So we set off, the buses dropped us further back along the coast. Maddy and I set off with Rani and Chloe. Nathan, who I naturally had my beady eye on, was with Zack and Connor ahead of us. I wanted to catch them up straight away, but I didn't want to rouse the suspicions of Rani and Chloe, who were still strangely against me making love happen. I can't think why they are like this. I couldn't make it look too obvious so I had to hop around nervously while Rani faffed about with her backpack and, by the time she'd got her neckscarf on right, we were nearly the last to set off except for Doug and Eddie. And no, Mr Trent hadn't noticed it yet.

It was beautiful watching the sun slowly go down over the sea, first shining silver and then the sky deepening in colour, turning pink and orange. I noticed that we had got fitter and with no neckscarf to cause me shame (accidentally on purpose left on the cabin floor) and with walking only on gentle sand dunes, it was not at all like our first hike, but actually enjoyable. As the light faded and the shadows lengthened, I found myself thinking that a two-hour walk was really no more than a stroll.

But I did not let the stunning views across the bay and the rhythmic sound of the waves distract me from my purpose.

'This is great, isn't it?' I sighed cheerfully.

'It is,' Chloe replied. 'It's so lovely here, so peaceful and quiet. Watching the nightfall. I wouldn't want to be to be here on my own though . . .'

'Don't be silly. There are loads of us wandering along this path. And Mr Trent, hero and fearless "dangerous criminal-searcher" is around too.'

'Yeah, I noticed Chantelle's not volunteering for anything any more.' Rani smiled smugly. 'She's realised she doesn't stand a chance . . . As if!'

'Miss Gwatkins is still trying though. I noticed she was keeping very close when we set off.'

'Like she stands a chance either,' Rani snorted.

'Well, I still feel love is in the air,' I said and began to do some lunging movements on the path and a few stretches.

'What the hell are you doing, Carrie?' Rani gasped.

I gave a long breath out in a casual type way. 'Whoooooh, I don't know, I think I feel like a bit of a run, you know, feel the wind in my hair type thing . . . What do you say, Maddy? You and me, have a bit of a sprint along the path, see if we can, um . . . catch up with the people in front . . .' I stretched my arm over my head and leaned right over. 'What do you say? Up for it?'

'Carrie!' Chloe was giggling. 'What are you on? You've never felt like a run in your life. Have a bit of a sprint?! Have you had a personality transplant or something?'

'Yeah, and what's all this bendy, springy stuff?' Rani sniggered. 'Where's that all coming from?'

I raised myself from a final lunge forward, stuck my nose in the air and shook my hair back from my face.

'I'm not talking to you two. I was asking Maddy. Maddy and I like running.'

Maddy was looking at me as if I'd lost my mind.

'So what do you say, Maddy, how about it, how about running for a bit?'

She put her head on one side, 'Well, OK-ay,' she said slowly. 'But are you sure? You remember . . .?'

And I knew she was going to refer to some of our early morning runs. This was ages and ages ago, at the beginning of term, when Maddy had first come to our school. Rani and I had decided to jog with her in the mornings to help her get fit. It turned out that she *was* the fit one. I do not care to remember clinging to a lamp post fighting for breath while Maddy looked on concerned. But I had to be loads fitter now after all this fresh air and exercise. I could certainly make it to Nathan anyway. They couldn't be that far ahead.

'Off you go then,' Rani chortled.

'Yes, off you go, Carrie, you little gazelle you.' Chloe began to make shooing movements. 'Fly, fly like the wind . . .'

Rani suddenly looked very serious and added, 'Be very careful about injuring yourself, Carrie.'

I gave her a sidelong glance.

'No! I mean it. I don't want to be the one who has to inform the Olympic Committee that you might not make the Games. They'll go mental.' And then they were both laughing so much they had to sit down.

I tossed my hair again. 'Come on, Maddy, ignore them. Let's go.'

Maddy shrugged her shoulders and we set off to the cries of Chloe and Rani: 'Good luck, Carrie! The nation's hopes are pinned on you!'

Now the thing I have discovered about running is this: at first it's very easy and then very, very soon it becomes a great deal harder. But I was determined to catch up with Nathan and so I gritted my teeth and tried to smile when Maddy kept asking me if I was all right. Never has the sight of the backs of Year Nine boys in the dusky light made anyone so happy.

With one last almighty effort I drew alongside Nathan, with Maddy completely relaxed and composed at my side.

'Hi,' I wheezed as I tried to get some breath back in my body.

Nathan looked startled. 'Hi. Whoah! Carrie, what's the matter? You look like a tomato.'

Year Nine boys have still got a lot to learn when it comes to women. I hope Maddy realises this.

I placed a steadying hand on Maddy's shoulder. 'No, no, I'm (pant, gasp) fine.'

'You sure?' Zack asked. 'You look like you're about to explode.'

See what I mean?

I wiped my brow. 'No, honestly I'm great. Just fancied a bit of a run. Phew! Invigorating! Think I'll wait for Rani and Chloe now though. Just sit up in the dunes for a moment. Experience nature type thing . . .'

Maddy took off her backpack. 'I'll wait with you then.'

'NO!' I think I might have said that a bit too loudly because everyone jumped, so I put on a more normal voice. 'No, honestly, you go on, Maddy. I, I . . . really will be fine. Just fancy a few moments, you know . . . to be *at one* with nature . . .'

I could see Maddy was reluctant to leave me.

'On my *own*, just fancy spending a few moments in solitude . . .'

Maddy frowned. 'Well, if you're sure . . . they did say *not* to leave anyone on their own . . .'

I nodded vigorously. 'Oh I'm sure, you know Rani and Chloe are just behind us, you go on with Nathan and . . . the others.' I frowned at Zack and Connor. It wasn't their fault they were there, but I hoped they would let Nathan and Maddy talk together and not keep interrupting or anything. What more could I do? I had tried my best. And I desperately needed to lie down and stop feeling like I was going to die.

Maddy set off reluctantly with the boys, but I was pleased to see, before she disappeared into the gloom, Nathan and her immediately falling into conversation. Success! Even Nathan and his mates thinking the real reason I wanted to be alone was to have a pee was worth it.

Talking of peeing.

I am going to get down from this bunk and go to the loo. And get a glass of water. All that writing about running has made me thirsty.

11.00 p.m.

I am back. As I climbed down from my bunk, Rani's sleeping form gave my already fragile nerves another major shock by suddenly reaching out and grabbing my ankle.

'What on earth did you do that for! Don't you think I've had enough terrorisation for one evening?'

She propped herself up on her elbows. 'I want to see the badger cubs. It's our last night. This is my only chance, my one and only chance. I've decided, I'm going to stay awake and creep out later. I asked Chantelle, she was a bit dim about where they are, but I think I know sort of where now.'

'Did you tell her you were planning to go and see them?'

'No way! I'm not an idiot.'

'Oh no, of course you're not; you're going out in the dark, into woods you don't know, to find a place you're not sure about . . . to look at badgers —'

Rani gazed sorrowfully at me and whispered, 'You've never understood my love of animals, have you, Carrie? If you knew how much this meant to me you would know why I have to go . . . I'm not asking you to come too, not after what you've been through this evening . . .'

'I'll come,' whispered Chloe, making us jump. 'I'd love to see them. Especially now I know the woods are safe.'

'Me too.' That was Maddy.

Well let them. Personally, I have had enough excitement to last me a lifetime.

So I wished them luck and crawled back up here to the safety of my bunk.

Let me get back to me sitting in the sand dune, by the side of the coastal path. By the time I had climbed up and made myself comfortable between the tufts of long, wiry grass, it was quite dark – only the moon hanging like a dim lantern high above me gave any light. Rani and Chloe were taking forever to get to me and it started to get cooler. I dragged off my backpack and felt rather sorry that I hadn't packed that stupid scarf. I got out my torch just in case I might need it. I kept one ear open to listen for Rani's voice coming along the pathway. And the time just went on and on and it got darker and darker and I'm ashamed to say I did find myself warbling 'All Things Bright and Beautiful' again in a reedy voice. Then I heard it. A rustle in the shrubs behind me. Close, and definitely not the wind blowing through the grass. Was it an animal? What sort of animal lives on a sand dune? I was trying to think of the answer to this when I heard it again and this time it was louder and if it was an animal it was a very big one. There was a booming in my chest and my mouth went dry. I didn't know whether to leap up and start shouting (if I could make my body do it) or to keep lying down low and hope that whoever it was hadn't seen me. My brain was racing, but I just couldn't move. I heard a scratching sound and the noise of someone moving through the grass towards me. I forced myself up to a crouch, ready to run. I managed to feel for my torch, pointed it at the source of the noise and flicked the switch. Nothing. The batteries had run out. Why oh why hadn't I changed them before we came out? And where on earth were Rani and Chloe? They should have gone past ages ago. I wanted to call out for them, but I was too scared. And then it started, very faint at first, like a sigh and then quickly it got more hoarse and more menacing. Someone was very, very close to me in the dark, and I could hear their breathing, rasping and hoarse, and getting so close to me now that I could almost feel the heat of their breath.

All I could think was 'It was all true'. I was crawling through the shrubby growth on the dune, and I realised it was just like Doug said – he'd waited and waited until he'd got one of us on our own. My feet started stumbling and I hurled myself down on to the path. I saw Rani and Chloe coming along the path just a short distance away from me. 'RUN!' I screamed, waving my arms. 'Run! It's him, it's the Breather! I heard him!'

'What are you talking about?' Rani shouted as she began to run towards me, but as she got closer she could see the expression on my face in her torchlight, and now, behind us we could hear someone crashing down the dune. That was enough for them. We fled along the path. Chloe found it in herself to start screaming and then we all did. We didn't stop shrieking and yelling until we crashed into Mrs McGuy and Mr Trent coming towards us. I have never been so grateful to see Mrs McG's solid, tweedy mass in my life.

'What on earth are you making such a racket about?' she

snapped. 'What kind of behaviour is that from young girls? It's bad enough that Mr Trent and I have had to come back to look for you. Why did you leave the path? Mr Trent was checking the rear of the group and he didn't see you, so he assumed you were ahead.'

'Mrs McGuy,' I gasped. 'We must run, I heard, I heard ... the *Breather*!'

Mrs Mc Guy's nostrils went on mega flare. 'Indeed! Well let me tell you, Carrie Henderson, I've had quite enough of these "Breather" shenanigans on this trip.'

'But he was *there*. I swear it. I heard him, in the bushes and he's after us ...'

Mrs McG shone her powerful torch down the pathway. 'And where is he then?'

'He must be hiding,' Chloe whispered. 'There honestly was someone chasing us, Mrs McGuy. We heard them.'

'Perhaps Mr Trent could go and look?' Rani asked, gazing up at her hero, but he didn't seem that keen on it somehow.

'There is no "Breather", girls,' he said. 'Just lively imaginations.'

'But we saw the newspaper clipping!' Rani protested.

'Ah yes, the newspaper clipping,' said Mrs McGuy. 'Well after our little drama last night and your tales of this dreadful villain stalking the cabins and the woods I took it upon myself to have a chat with young Mr Brennan on the subject.'

'So you know it's true,' Chloe groaned.

'If you silly creatures had taken it upon yourselves to look more closely, you would have seen that it wasn't genuine. Simply something he and his friends had created on a computer, to look like a newspaper cutting. The whole story is a complete fabrication to frighten gullible girls.'

'But Mrs McGuy, there was someone in the bushes, I honestly and truly did hear them.'

'And Carrie would never lie about something like that,' Rani added. 'And we heard someone chasing us too.'

'I'm quite sure there was someone in the bushes, ladies – I think you may be interested to know that you are not the only people who are straggling behind. Doug Brennan and Eddie Hope are also missing. Have you seen them?'

'They were behind us right at the start, Mrs McGuy,' Chloe offered. 'Then Eddie caught up with us and said he'd seen lots of rabbits and did we want to see them as there were loads of babies – so Rani and I stayed behind with him, waiting and waiting up in the dunes for these rabbits that never appeared and Doug went ahead.'

'That was just after Maddy and Carrie ran off. Then, when we said we couldn't hang about in the dunes any longer, Eddie said he'd like to stay a bit more, so we went on ahead . . . but I don't know what happened to Doug . . . Oooh, er . . .' Rani clapped her hand to her mouth.

Mrs McGuy nodded. '*Indeed*. Right now, you girls come back with me and Mr Trent will pick up the "Breather" and his accomplice.'

Rani commented on our walk back that Mr T still has not mentioned her neckscarf.

According to Tess and Cara, Gemma had not been at all happy to see Maddy arriving at the beach with Nathan. She had sat looking mopey and miserable, rubbing her ankle in an agonised way, until he came over and sat with her. What bad luck was that for Nathan, to feel responsible for that injury? Gemma had made sure that everyone knew it wasn't a sprain that was going to heal very quickly either.

Doug and Eddie were not allowed to come to the barbecue as punishment, but that punishment is but nothing compared to the punishment that they will get from us when we see them again. How could Doug do that to me? He is the lowest form of pond life. Even Mr Trent, who loves all creatures and says there is good in everyone, would surely struggle to find the good in Doug Brennan.

I wonder if I can sue for years of my life lost due to suffering extreme stress?

I can hear stirring in the bunk below. Rani is getting out of her bunk and has started to get dressed. So have the others. They are all talking in excited whispers.

Let me see, how much do I want to see baby badgers?

CARRIE'S TIP: • • • • • • • • • • • • • • • • • • •

If stress and life in general has brought your skin out in spots, try this carrot mask – it's great for blemishes.

Either grate a raw carrot very finely and mash up, or boil one for a few minutes and mash. Pat the mask all over the spotty areas and leave on for fifteen to twenty minutes. Rinse and pat dry.

Chapter 19

Monday 10.40 a.m.

I am on the coach. I am sitting next to Rani. She is leaning against the window with her arms crossed and with a very tight-lipped expression. She is not the only one. Most of the girls in Year Nine look the same.

'Are you going to put why?' she has just said, nudging me. (Even in a sulk she's still nosey.)

Of course I am.

I did decide to go with them to the woods.

In the end, the experience of observing the badgers in their natural habitat seemed too good to miss.

'HAH!'

(That was Rani just now, by the way.)

'Do you want to write this?' I have asked her.

She has shaken her head.

So this is what happened.

We all crept out across the grass to the woods. We didn't put our torches on. Four girls waving torches in the dark might look like a good impression of motorway traffic coming straight at you. Tiny bit *noticeable*. Like from outer space.

Rani says we then went on a 'wild badger' chase.

We kept going round in circles in the moonlight, until at last we came to a clearing and Rani said she was sure this was it. She made us creep like mice through the wood and not put our torches on, as she didn't want to scare them away.

'HAH!'

Stop saying that, Rani, you're making me jump.

Rani then held up one hand and put the finger of the other on her lips and we all stopped moving and it was totally quiet – just the sound of the wind, a bit like when I was in the dunes. And then we heard it. Someone in the bushes nearby, and some heavy breathing.

Now Rani wants me to say *specifically* that it was me who whispered, 'Not again! Do they think we're totally dumb? Doug and Eddie must have seen us come out of our cabin and followed us.' Maybe it *was* me. I can't remember.

Rani has just stated firmly, 'It was.'

We crept a bit nearer to the rustling. Chloe opened her mouth and I knew she was going to shout out at them that we knew they were there. But I believed I had a better idea.

'HAH!'

For goodness' sake! Will you stop with the 'Hah' thing, please!

So I put my finger on my lips and mimed with my other hand a running, *leaping* motion towards the bush.

So we all got into our starting positions and then I hissed, 'Ready, steady, GO!' and we all raced towards the bushes, yelling at the tops of our voices, and hurled ourselves in the air in order to dive from the very highest height on top of our prey.

Rani has dropped her head in her hands next to me.

'Go on, then.' She is nudging me with her elbow now. 'Say what you said when we had all picked ourselves off the heap.'

Very well. This is what I said. No, I didn't *say*, what I *gasped* was:

'MR TRENT!'

And then Chloe shouted, 'CHANTELLE!'

And after Mr Trent had got his wind back and staggered up from the forest floor, he said he couldn't imagine what we were doing out in the woods at this time of night and we all just gawped at him in shock. It was Chantelle who spoke first. Brushing the undergrowth from her skirt, explaining that she and Mr Trent were lying in a special hiding place in wait for the badgers.

This was met with raised eyebrows and silent disbelief. Actually not quite silent. I think it was Maddy who let out a short bark of laughter.

Mr Trent started nodding vigorously. 'Yes, that's right. But I don't think they're out tonight!' He then stood up very straight and said briskly, 'And now I must take you girls *straight* back to your cabins. I don't know *what* Mrs McGuy is going to make of this . . .' I wasn't quite sure if he meant in regards to himself or to us.

And on the way back he started talking about the beauty of the nocturnal animal world and the nightlife of our furry woodland creatures. But he had lost his audience. Only Chantelle was listening, tottering merrily alongside him. 'So Rani,' he ventured, 'are you coming out for that last look at the sun rising tomorrow?' He looked at his watch. 'Er, or should I say, today?'

Rani's nose went up into the air. 'I don't *think* so,' she replied snootily pulling her scarf more tightly around her neck.

'Great neckscarf. It's like the ones they have at Rainbow Ridge,' he added.

Rani closed her eyes as if in pain.

11.55 a.m.

Still on the coach.

Have had my packed lunch. Not as good as Mum's. I am actually looking forward to seeing Mum and Dad very much. I wonder how Ned's audition went? And soon I'm going to be seeing Jack. Even with all the drama of the last few days I haven't stopped thinking about him and looking forward to seeing him. I can't wait. I sent him a text as soon as I got my phone. We're meeting up as soon as I get back. Mum's picking us up and dropping us off at the Coffee Bean so we can see each other straight away. Sometimes Mum is very, very kind and understanding.

I hope she will be kind and understanding about what happened at Baxted Hall. Mrs McGuy did go mad with us, but it was clear she was even angrier with Mr Trent's tale of badger watching with Chantelle. She did do him the favour of keeping between him and a red-faced, glaring George, until she had delivered him safely on to the coach. We could all see Chantelle waving at us from the reception window. I think everyone agreed that it was just as well we were leaving today. The tale of Mr Trent's fall from grace was all over the Hall. You know that saying, 'Hell hath no fury like a woman scorned'? Well, that was most of 9M if the cold-shouldering and coolness in the air was anything to go by. He had to run the gauntlet of the whole year as he made his way to police the back of the coach. After our trip here, some motorists had taken the coach number and complained about some of the more interesting notices pressed up against the window for their perusal.

Jet and Melanie are sitting behind us. Jet is in five-inch heels and hot pants and Melanie is in a gold lamé mini. They are covered in thick make-up. It is their way of making a protest. I couldn't believe they had packed that stuff, but Jet said it was always best to be ready for a change of mood clothes-wise – and obviously the events of last night had brought on a complete about-turn.

'You're welcome to the title of Miss Beautiful Spirit,' she said primly to Rani as she settled down in her seat.

I had to feel sorry for Mr Trent as he walked past all those silent, judgemental faces. And none more so than Miss Gwatkins. I noticed she did not save him a place this time. Talk about a fallen idol.

Rani is leaning her head against the window now and staring out at the motorway traffic. I can tell she is bitterly disappointed.

I hope Maddy isn't too disappointed. A few seats in front of us, Gemma is still sitting next to Nathan; she's made him leap up every five minutes to do little errands for her. 'I'm a little bit thirsty, Nathan, do you mind?' or 'Could you just reach up and get my fleece, Nathan, the air conditioning is very chilly . . .'. He's like her slave. Zack and Connor are sitting further back on the bus; I think they must have given up on Nathan ever breaking free. She's already talking about how Nathan will need to help her carry her books at school and come and keep her company in the holidays as she won't really be able to do very much and, oh dear, she did have so much planned that is now ruined, etc., etc. We've still got hours to go on this coach and I don't think I can stand listening to her much more.

12.45 p.m.
I didn't have to.

Jet and Melanie got bored not being able to entertain passing motorists and decided to get out their mobiles. They had been returned to us by a smiling Chantelle this morning. After a few button-pushing beeps, Jet gave out a shriek that made me leap three feet off my seat.

'How the hell did that get on there?'

'I don't know, show me.' There was the sound of a slight tussle over the camera phone.

'I don't believe it, it's Chantelle!' Melanie sounded furious. 'The bloody cheek of it – she must have filmed herself on your bloody mobile while she had them all in reception. You should sue —'

'Shut up, Melanie!' Jet hissed. 'Listen to what she's saying!'

And although Rani and I strained our ears our very hardest we couldn't make out what it was.

We didn't have to wait long to find out though.

After they had played whatever it was through a few times, Jet slid out of her chair, holding her mobile aloft and shimmied past us along the aisle to where Nathan and Gemma were sitting in front of us. She leaned lazily against the seat and gave Gemma a chilly smile.

'Hi, Gemma.'

Gemma looked back at her with equal enthusiasm. 'Hi.' And turned to continue her conversation Nathan.

Jet picked a piece of fluff off her halter-neck and gazed around in a casual fashion before saying into the air, 'Must have been tough for you, with your poorly foot, not being able to get around and everything. You must be in *loads* of pain . . .'

Gemma stared back calmly at her. 'Yes, I am, Jet, but I really don't want to make too much of a fuss about it.'

'Nooo, I'll just bet you don't. But you've been *so* lucky to have

Nathan to look after you, haven't you? He feels so responsible for your injury and all . . .'

Nathan flushed.

'Nathan has been very caring, which is no more than I would expect in the circumstances . . . He's not the sort of boy to desert a girl in her time of need.' Through the gap in the seats I saw Gemma place her hand on his and give him a sickly smile.

Rani made her puking face.

'Yes, now what exactly *are* those circumstances? As far as I saw it, you fell backwards coming off the coach and you sort of collapsed in a heap clutching your ankle.'

Nathan groaned, 'Jet, do we have to go over this again? I know what I did . . .'

'Oh but did you?' Jet's eyes glittered. 'Did you? Isn't that an *interesting* question?'

'What d'you mean?' Nathan looked puzzled.

'Well, Nathan, I shall tell you. Our little friend Chantelle turns out to have been not as clueless as we all thought. In fact, she turned out to be quite the detective. And she's recorded a most interesting message on my phone. Do you remember last night when Gemma had to stay behind with her while we did the coastal walk?'

'What about it?'

Jet switched on her mobile and turned up the sound very loud so everyone sitting around could hear. 'Let's let Chantelle tell it, shall we?'

I couldn't see the picture but just about everyone on the bus could hear what she was saying, 'Hi, girls, Chantelle speaking,' – giggles – 'but you can see that for yourselves can't you, silly me.

Sorry to hijack your phone, Jet – nice touch to put your name in diamante on the back – but I thought you might like to know something. You know last night your friend with the sprained ankle was supposed to be staying in reception with me, before I drove her down to the beach for the barbecue? You know who I mean, the girl who treated me like I was something that came off the bottom of her shoe? She said she wanted to get a bit of fresh air and so I said, "Yeah, why not?" Give me five minutes' peace from running around after her. And as soon as she'd hobbled out, I thought, bloody hell, what if anything happens to her with her bad ankle and all, she'd be the first to complain and get me into trouble. And I'm supposed to be looking after her and everything. What might people say about me letting her go off on her own and not offering to help or nothing? So I have a look out the window to check she's OK and there is Miss Hobble-Ankle running fast as you like across the grass to the boys' cabin. I couldn't believe it so I grabbed this phone, went to the window and started filming. So there she is. I feel bad for that nice boy she gets to run around after her all the time when she's not getting me to do it. She obviously went to have a good snoop around in his cabin as well. I wasn't going to say a word, you know, having been in a bit of trouble lately with blabbing a bit too much about stuff, but that boy was always dead polite to me and he needs to know he's being conned. In the end I just thought you should know. By the way, *loved* the hot-pants-and-heels, girls. What were you girls like with your baggy shorts and floppy sandals, I don't know! Taraaaa! Enjoy the other movie on here.'

'Chantelle's lying,' Gemma hissed. 'She's lying because she wants to make trouble. Look how much trouble she made for poor Mr Trent.'

There was a brief silence as Chantelle's movie rolled. Nobody was buying Gemma's injury any more now.

Nathan turned to face Gemma, who had gone quite white.

'I don't understand . . .' His voice was strained and confused. 'I mean, I can't get my head round this. *What's been going on*? You've been *faking* being in pain? You went through my stuff . . . what, are you crazy? And *why*? Why would you do that?'

I could have told him the answer to that one. 'To find anything, any information at all that might help her keep you.'

I was right about not getting on the wrong side of Jet. It's very dangerous. She slunk triumphantly back to her seat. Nathan got up, ignoring Gemma's protests and meandered in a daze down the coach till he sank on to an empty seat across the aisle from Zack and Connor. Zack wordlessly offered him a battered cheese sandwich. Connor handed him his lemonade can. Nathan took a swig and sighed. You could see the tension begin to ebb away from his face. He raised the can and said, 'Ta'. None of them said anything else. Zack punched his arm. Such is the way with boys.

It has been very quiet ever since.

I think there are a lot of people on this coach coping with very difficult emotions.

I miss Jack.

3.05 p.m.

Nearly home. Thank goodness.

Even thinking about Jack is not stopping me churning over the events since Mr Trent got here. I know the first thing he did was close down my business empire, I know I was rude about his 'Hello clouds, hello sky' personality and drippy way of talking. I know I never got why almost everyone else loved him with a love that was true, but it's not exactly fair to treat him like he's the worst man on the planet.

He taught us loads of stuff about recycling and caring for the environment and, thanks to him, Mum has agreed to the special bins coming for recycling clothes and shoes. And we can have the clothes swap next term and Dad's cycling to work instead of getting into his car ... LOADS of stuff. In fact I'm going to tell him. I'm going to walk down the aisle to the back of the bus and tell him. I don't care what anyone else thinks.

I THINK IT'S THE RIGHT THING TO DO.

Rani is giving me *a look*. But I don't care. We did learn loads from him. I can't forget about that. OK, he said he liked women to be as nature intended – OK, Chantelle didn't *exactly* fit that description, but do you know, underneath the boobs and the high heels, she was actually a really nice person. She didn't have to leave that message.

Rani has turned her head away and is gazing out of the window again. I am going to write her a message in big letters now and stick it in front of her nose. It will say:

NOBODY'S PERFECT.

NOT EVEN YOU.

I'm off to make my speech now before we get to school. I won't get another chance. Mrs McGuy says Miss Gooding is back (on crutches) tomorrow and this will be Mr Trent's last day.

4.00 p.m.

Sitting in the Coffee Bean waiting for Jack. Mum dropped us off early. I am writing this to stop myself from constantly staring at the door and so I don't look too over-excited.

I did it. I swayed down to the back of the coach. He looked a bit apprehensive at first. As I went down the aisle I realised that everyone was watching me and suddenly I wondered whether it was such a good idea after all, but I knew I had to do it whatever.

So I just went up and said, 'Mr Trent, I know this is your last day, but I wanted to say before you go, thanks for teaching me a lot about stuff I didn't know. You made me aware of lots of things I've never thought about before and because of that some real changes have taken place in our school and also in my house. I didn't realise that anyone could do their bit to help, whatever their age. So, er . . .' I was aware of lots of ears all around listening intently to every word I said. 'That's it really, thank you. Thanks a lot.'

He had gone quite red. 'Oh, yes, well, thank you, Carrie. That's er . . . very nice of you to say so.'

And then we were pulling into the road by our school so I had to run back to my seat and start to gather my stuff up. Everyone was staring at me. Rani had a weird expression on her face I couldn't work out.

We all trudged off the coach and had to hang around outside for our bags to be excavated. Maddy went up first. 'Thanks, Mr Trent.' Then Sasha, then Chloe, Cara and Tess and then everyone went up, including Rani. Even the boys said, 'Goodbye and thanks.'

Rani has just nudged me. She wants me to write something.

I have said depends what it is.

She says to write down that Rani said, 'Carrie did the right thing'. She said I was brave too. Now didn't I say something before about me and braveness?

Rani says don't push it.

RANI'S TIP: ● ● ● ● ● ● ● ● ● ● ● ● ● ● ● ● ● ● ●

A drop of lemon juice on the tongue can help your breath smell sweeter. Lemons are also good for rubbing on your teeth to whiten them. If you can bear it.

Chapter 20

Then Jack strolled into the Coffee Bean – all black jeans and hands in pockets. I confess I gave him quite a big hug. He didn't seem to mind at all. In fact it seemed very much a two way kind of hug, but of course that was any pretence at cool gone. I despair of myself sometimes.

We told the boys about our ordeal. They laughed.

'You know I really can't see what's so funny about that,' Rani said, crisply.

'Me neither,' Chloe agreed. 'It's actually emotional abuse and I think we could sue.'

'I don't know what you're complaining about.' I put down my hot chocolate. 'Who was that girl sitting in the dark warbling "All Things Bright and Beautiful" in a bush while Doug Brennan sniggered at my fear? Not you. Me. Me. My terror was cheap entertainment for Doug and Eddie.'

'Hey! We had terror too you know,' Chloe protested.

I pursed my lips and shook my head. 'Not in the same league.'

But it was hard to be really mad with Doug or anyone today because Jack was sitting next to me and I felt happy, happy, happy.

Unlike Jennifer Cooper who was sitting further up the café, tapping her fingernails on the table and looking thunderous. Obviously Mr Wonderful – Chris Jones – was a no-show.

'When is she going to realise that he is so not worth it?' Chloe sighed. Tom put his arm around her. 'Sometimes people just refuse to face the facts.'

'Like Gemma.'

'I'm trying to work out whether it's mad or sort of romantic,' Rani mused.

'Mad!' I shrieked.

'But she did it because she lurved him, didn't she?'

'She thought she did it because she lurved him, but that was no way to treat someone you care about. You wouldn't do that to someone you really loved, properly.' And I'm sorry to say I found myself going a bit too pink when I said that, what with Jack sitting right beside me.

'I agree,' Chloe nodded. 'And it's true, sometimes you have to accept things aren't going to happen between you and somebody and move gracefully on to wait for someone who feels the same way you do.'

'And sometimes if you wait,' I said, 'circumstances can change and things might happen.'

'God, you're not still thinking about Maddy and Nathan, are you?' Rani and Jack groaned in unison.

I tapped the side of my nose. 'I have my reasons for feeling pretty confident in that area, oh yes. It was well and truly over after what she did. Some people are now free agents. But I will say no more.'

And then Maddy appeared at our table. Her eyes were shining and she was bursting with brilliant mood vibes. I gave the table a triumphant look.

'Maddy! What's happened?' Rani asked. 'You look like you have just won the lottery!'

She blushed, beaming down at us.

'Well sit down and tell us all about it.' Chloe began shuffling up the seat.

Maddy blushed even more. 'Er, I can't.' She looked back at the queue at the counter. All our eyes swivelled to follow her gaze.

To my astonishment, Joe Carter was holding aloft two coffees and indicating a free table with his blond head.

'Wh-at?' I managed to croak.

'You on a date-ette with Joe? Maddy, you are a dark horse,' Jack said, grinning.

'I thought he was going out with Steph,' I said, trying to sound relaxed.

'He ended it when we were away. We'd been seeing a bit of each other for a while, just as friends. He's mad about American football and he came round a few times to watch with me because I like it too. Anyway,' she laughed, 'it's not going to be a surprise to *you*, Carrie, is it? I thought I hadn't let on to a soul that I liked him but Carrie somehow knew. She must be a bit psychic, or just *hugely* emotionally intelligent or something, mustn't she?' She smiled around the table.

'Absolutely,' Jack agreed, putting his arm around me. 'That's our Carrie; *hugely* emotionally intelligent. Finger completely on the pulse of the love department.'

'And she was so discreet,' Maddy continued. 'She never let on to a single soul.'

'She's amazing.' Rani shook her head. 'Truly amazing.'

Maddy disappeared to sit with Joe and as my astonished gaze followed her, I spotted Nathan standing by Jennifer's table and obviously shyly asking her if he could join her. She paused for a moment, looked into his hopeful face, shrugged gracelessly and made room for him.

I am going to give matchmaking a rest for a while. Mum is calling me downstairs to eat.

8.00 p.m.

So great to be home with my lovely, lovely mum and dad, who I appreciate all the more after being away. Dad is looking healthier already and actually *thanked* me for persuading him to get on his bike. Mum assures me they stuck to nearly all the green rules. She made a homecoming supper of my favourite: shepherd's pie and peas.

I am even pleased to see Ned. He is being so nice to me, it is quite spooky. He keeps saying things like 'Great to see you, sis' which is not like him at all. It's almost like he feels guilty about something, but the only thing I can think of is that all our holiday plans are still on hold while we wait to hear about this stupid film part. Mum says we may even have to go to stay near the studios in Buckinghamshire for a few weeks. Terrific. But totally ruining my summer is not usually the sort of thing that would bother Ned. It must be something else. Everything in my room is in order; my CDs are all where I left them . . .

I asked him about his audition in London and he just shrugged and said, 'I dunno. They'll let me know.' But when I spoke to Mum she said she thought they liked him a lot. In a minute I am going back down to watch telly in the bosom of my family.

Ned has just popped in with a cup of tea and a packet of

Minstrels. He put them down on my dressing table ignoring my speechless expression. As he got to the door he turned. 'Sis?'

'Mmm? What? This is great tea, Ned, but you didn't have to bring it up, I'm coming down to watch telly with my loving family now.'

Ned started. 'What, sis? You don't want to watch telly tonight, you must be knackered.'

'I am, that's why I want to watch telly.'

'But you never watch *Spy Camera*, ever!'

'Is that what's on? I'm not bothered. I'll watch anything tonight.'

'Why don't we talk instead, I mean for instance – what would you do if someone gave you two hundred and fifty quid?'

'Like if I'd got a clip on *Spy Camera* you mean? What would I do?! Wow! That's a weird question. You're very weird altogether today, Ned – what's up?'

'You could buy your LA Alpha tickets, couldn't you? You really want to go. I mean being able to go to that concert would be your total dream, wouldn't it? I think if you had two hundred and fifty pounds, that would just about wipe out anything, er . . . troubling, that might have happened in your life, wouldn't it? Like, wipe the slate clean so to speak . . .'

'What are you on about, Ned? Wipe what slate clean? And no, Ned. It's the strangest thing, but I have been on an enlightening journey this past week and although there was a burger-selling time when I would have spent most of my two hundred and fifty pounds on LA Alpha tickets, that's not what I would spend money on now. Nor would Chloe – we were discussing it while we were away.'

'What would you do with it?'

'We decided that if we managed by some miracle to get hold of some money we'd donate it to Jim's school so they can buy a really good henhouse for those battery chickens they want to rescue. Give them a good life pottering around free in the field by the school. Now if you'll excuse me I would like to get past to go downstairs to be with my beloved parents.'

9.00 p.m.

I don't know what Ned was going to say next because the phone rang and the next minute Mum was shrieking up the stairs for Ned and then all thoughts of telly disappeared because NED GOT THE PART! When Mum said it was a school programme that wasn't quite the whole story. It's a programme about a school – my favourite series on TV: *Hollywood High*. Mum kept it quiet because she didn't want hysteria in the school. They were going to shoot Ned's part as a visiting English kid in the Buckinghamshire studios, but after everyone had seen him in London they want to make his part a bit bigger. And that means he has to go to Los Angeles. And after a long discussion in the kitchen and several more phone calls, Dad has decided we're *all* going to go. Huzzah! It is as Mum feared. I am hysterical.

And guess who are the stars? Serenity Blue and Darren Inigo. Double Huzzah!

I must phone Rani straight away.

9.45 p.m.

She rang *me*. All cagey and not at all sounding like Rani.

'Hi, Carrie,' she began cautiously.

'Rani! The most incredible news! I'm not going to be having a miserable summer with nothing to do except worry if Jack cares enough to still want to go out with me when he comes back. Ned got the part!'

And I told her all the news, but even though she was obviously thrilled for me I could still detect something in her voice that told me something wasn't right.

'What is it, Rani, you sound a bit peculiar.'

'You didn't watch any telly this evening, did you?'

'No, I was going to watch *Spy Camera*, but we got the Ned phone call and then it was just pandemonium.'

'Mmmm.'

'Why do you mention it? Did you watch it?'

'Mmmmm.'

'Was it any good?'

'Well, that sort of depends on your perspective.'

'What are you on about, Rani?'

'You know you said Ned had been running around with a camera acting strangely . . .'

'Oh my God, you don't say he actually got one of his sad little "ball hitting head in the garden" clips on it, do you?' (I had eventually worked it out.)

'No-oo. Not one of *those* clips.'

'What then?'

'OK, Carrie, I'm going to tell you because, Lord knows, you're going to find out anyway – *Spy Camera* having viewing figures of several million . . . and I want you to remember that you *did* say you wanted to be in a romantic film.'

'Go on.' I felt an ominous chill descend on me.

'Do you remember the night we camped in your garden?'

'Ye-es.'

'Do you remember when you were dancing around and we're larking about and you were shouting something and then you fell into the wheelbarrow.'

'God, please tell me no . . . Where was he filming from?'

'Looks like the view from his bedroom window.'

'Remind me, Rani, what exactly was I shouting at the top of my voice?'

'Are you sure you want to hear it?'

'Go on. I have to know the worst. Prepare for my life being ruined.'

Rani took a deep breath. 'Well it starts with you dancing around . . .'

'Do I have a sprig of parsley up my nose?'

''Fraid so . . . and you are sort of singing a little song, you know the one you made up that night . . .'

'Can you hear the exact words on the clip?'

'I think I have to say in all honesty, yes, they are quite distinct.'

'Remind me.'

Rani cleared her throat. 'You have to imagine you dancing around with a jumper on your head to get the full effect, you know . . . but here goes . . .

'I love, I love

I love Jack forever

He's a seriously great kisser and brilliantly clever

But the really big question that's bothering me today is

Does he, does he, feel the same way?
Does he, does he, feel the same way?'

I couldn't bring myself to speak at first so Rani said helpfully, 'He may not have seen it, Carrie.'

But we both knew that even if he hadn't, someone would be calling him right now to let him know. I just couldn't bear to talk any more. I kept thinking about everything we'd said about people deluding themselves that people liked them and acting crazy. Would Jack think that about me? Was he trying to get through while I was talking to Rani to tell me what a fool I'd made of myself? Will I ever hear from him again? Why should he want to go out with a girl who has just made a complete idiot of herself on national TV?

'But the really big question that's bothering me today is
Does he, does he, feel the same way?'

This is the worst moment of my life.

10.00 p.m.

I was sitting here on the floor with my mobile in my hand. In deep shock.

I heard footsteps trying to creep past my door.

'NED! GET IN HERE THIS MINUTE!'

My bedroom door creaked open a fraction and Ned's eye appeared in the tiny crack.

'NED . . .'

My text alert went off. It was from Jack.

'NED, YOU STAY RIGHT THERE! DON'T YOU DARE MOVE!'

I read it. It was just two words.

He does.

I looked up at Ned. He put his head on one side and grinned nervously.

'Cluck?'

EVERYONE'S TIP: ●●●●●●●●●●●●●●●●●●●
The best, bestest, best beauty aid for any girl is totally natural and doesn't cost a penny. Smile at someone!

www.piccadillypress.co.uk

☆ The latest news on forthcoming books

☆ Chapter previews

☆ Author biographies

☆ Fun quizzes

☆ Reader reviews

☆ Competitions and fab prizes

☆ Book features and cool downloads

☆ And much, much more . . .

Log on and check it out!

Piccadilly Press